Seventy Summers

The Story of An Extraordinary Friendship

BOOK ONE:

Confidence

A Life/Business Fable by
ANDY STANGENBERG
with Ann Wilson

Steve Silananda
July 31, 2019

Seventy Summers
Copyright © 2018 by Andy Stangenberg

ISBN 978-1-7328131-0-6

Printed in USA by 48HrBooks (www.48HrBooks.com)

Cover illustration by Alisha Sickler-Brunelli

Dedicated to My Daughters:

Piper Macy Hoppe
We miss you every day.

Emmanuella Desirée Xin Ting
You were sent to rescue us.

We love you both so much!

"Confidence is the gradual building process that supports our development from childhood into adulthood, in every aspect of life—relationships, career, academics, sports, and hobbies. We gain confidence with every little successful step as we acquire skills. Once we achieve the high level of continued success we call "mastery"—and it takes a LOT of practice—we can use our confidence to further push boundaries, be bold, take risks, and instill confidence in others for their personal development. No matter how skilled or successful we become, it's important to stay humble and not let confidence transform into arrogance."

– Manuel Deisen
General Manager
Hotel Luxury Market

"Confidence is the instinctive ability to trust yourself—your knowledge, your life experiences—and know the decisions you make and the actions you take are fundamentally sound. It's the ability to expeditiously decide next steps, recognizing time is not your friend, while maintaining the agility to change direction."

– Scott Allen
General Manager
Hyatt Corporation

"Your experience tells you what to do; confidence allows you to do it."

– Steve LoGiudice
COO/GM, The Club at Ibis
West Palm Beach, Florida

"Being confident requires a balance of dignity, respect, determination, and humility. You can see this clearly in those who embrace success and failure equally as learning experiences and who can readily and genuinely say they are sorry when they are wrong. Confident people respect the experience and wisdom of the team and willingly ask others, "What do you think?", secure in the knowledge that ideas offered may be better than their own. In a business environment where quick thinking, a calming attitude, and the ability to take control in any situation are essential to success, confidence is demonstrated by those who genuinely and authentically accept who they are and what they have to offer."

> – *David Nadelman*
> *Area Vice President and*
> *General Manager*
> *Hyatt Corporation*

"Confidence in oneself is being assured of the outcome as well as the manner in which you will get there."

> – *Tom J. Voss*
> *Managing Director*
> *Fairmont Hotels & Resorts*
> *Austin, Texas*

"Genuine confidence is having the humility to know how much you don't know, the bravery to fail, and the unwavering, underlying purpose of advancing the human spirit . . . all the while knowing you'll never be worse off than where you started."

> – *Doug Sears*
> *General Manager*
> *Hyatt Corporation*

"Sports teaches great lessons about confidence. Getting good at any-thing is part nature and part knowledge. You can always compensate for the natural component, however small, through learning. Then it's up to the individual to practice, practice, practice for as long as it takes to become a master of the skill. That mastery creates trust in yourself, and that in turn gives you confidence."

> – *Rene Van Camp*
> *Head of Food & Beverage*
> *InterContinental Hotels Group,*
> *Europe*

ACKNOWLEDGMENTS

A special **Thank You** goes out to the following people. I learned through them who I am and who I would like to be, and they continue to guide me on the path to getting there. Some are part of my life today; others are with me now in spirit only.

My grandparents, Guenter and Elfride Hoppe. You stood by my side when I needed you most, and you never gave up on me. Thank you for your unconditional love and for an amazing childhood. I miss you.

My wife, Andrea. You are an inspiration to me, always. I'm grateful for your unfailing support and blessed to have you in my life. I would marry you all over again.

My daughter, Emmanuella (LaLa). You show me every day that bravery and strength are not just words but values to live by. You enrich my life, and I'm so proud to be the father of such a wonderful and kind child.

My mom, Eva. You made sure I had the opportunities I needed to become the person I wanted to be and to make a difference. You have always shown me that creativity is not a thing but rather a wondrous experience of discovering and expressing my imagination.

Ann Wilson. You are an amazing person, and I'm so glad to have met you and had the chance to work with you. What a journey it has been from many years ago when we started this project to bringing *Seventy Summers* to life today! Your wisdom, talent, and advice as editor have added so much to this book. I could not have done it without you. My deepest appreciation, and I'm looking forward to *Seventy Summers, Book Two*.

In addition, I offer a heartfelt "handshake" to these leaders in the field of self-development, whose work has influenced and inspired me:

Dr. Wayne Dyer

He has been my "coach," through his writings and teachings, for so many years. He made this world a better place, one person at a time. Rest in peace.

Tony Robbins

The strength of his words and presence in his seminars and books continue to help people make powerful changes in their lives. I'm grateful for his ongoing inspiration.

Zig Ziglar

Where would the world be without the wisdom and humor of the great Zig Ziglar? His sayings and writings have touched me—and so many, many others—and made us laugh, think, and take action. My respect for him and his contributions is enormous, and I regret he is no longer with us.

John C. Maxwell

The messages in his books on leadership are powerful and inspiring. His works have had a significant impact on my career and in my life.

Peter Dale Wimbrow

Composer, radio artist, and writer, Mr. Wimbrow is best known for his world-famous poem "The Guy in the Glass," which he wrote in 1934. I came across this unforgettable piece when I was researching *Seventy Summers*, and I thank his family for allowing me to include part of the poem here.

Mike Buscemi

His poem "The Average Child" was first presented at the 1979 National Parent Teacher Association conference. Thank you, Mike, for allowing me to make it part of this book. Your moving and thought-provoking words are as powerful and relevant today as they were forty years ago.

CONTENTS

Prologue

Though it was clear the tall, gangly man standing at the head of the boardroom table had finished speaking, none of the senior executives of Hoppe Enterprises uttered a word. They sat motionless, not quite understanding what had transpired over the past ten hours, or how a stranger could have had such a profound impact on them.

The man had touched the very core of their being, giving them back things they had lost over the years—the right to feel valued and important, the freedom to imagine and dream. He had caused them to fall back in love with who they truly were and to realize their individual capabilities and strengths as if for the first time. They were awakened from the illusion they had been living and so were forever changed. That, they knew, would alter not only the course of their entire company, but the rest of their lives. And it had only taken him a day.

The speaker glanced at the wall-mounted clock, which displayed 5:08 p.m. "My best to you all," he said, gathering up his rumpled trench coat and dropping his vintage brown fedora onto his head. "Time for me to fly.

"You may not recall much of the story I've told you today, but remember this above everything else: success is a matter of opinion—*your* opinion. It's the sum of self-expectation, self-confidence, and how you choose to be in the world. Like truth, success is in the eye of the beholder. That means *you* get to define it, not have it defined for you."

He looked around the table, holding each person's gaze for a few seconds with his keen eyes before saying in a soft but powerful voice, "Ladies and gentlemen, it has been a privilege. Farewell. And who knows, maybe someday we will meet again."

Then, smiling, he swung the trench coat over his narrow shoulders, tipped the hat in a mini-salute, pulled open the frosted-glass conference room door and was gone as if he never existed.

It took the group a few seconds to register his abrupt exit, at which point they simultaneously jumped to their feet and charged toward the door. They wanted to shake his hand and thank him, to say good-bye, and, most importantly, find out who in the heck he was, where he came from and whether he would be back.

Mrs. Tutwiler, the Hoppe Enterprises meeting concierge, was seated at her usual perch behind the imposing carved wood-and-marble welcome desk just outside the conference room. She almost fell off her chair when the heavy glass door flew open and eight executives stormed toward her.

"Where did he go?" demanded Karl Ruttner, the senior vice president of marketing.

"Who?" a bewildered Mrs. Tutwiler replied nervously, as if she were being questioned on the witness stand.

"Dalton—what was his last name?" Ruttner gasped in exasperation to Michelle Beckwith, the head of human resources, who was leaning in next to him. She shrugged her shoulders. He turned back to Mrs. Tutwiler. "You know, the man who just came out of the conference room. Tall, slender, round glasses, beat-up khaki raincoat."

"I'm sorry?" Mrs. Tutwiler said, fumbling with her reading spectacles and looking from side to side as if searching for the stranger herself.

The executives hovered around the desk like bees at a hive. "You must have seen him. He literally just left the conference room. Walked out that door and must have passed right by your desk."

"I'm sorry, Mr. Ruttner. I haven't left this desk for the past four hours. I didn't see a single person walk by in all that time and for sure did not see anyone come out of the conference room. I would have noticed that. I'm sorry," she said again.

* * * *

The elegant older lady paused in her story, chuckling with delight.

"Did he really keep them there without a break from dawn to almost dark?" I asked.

"I believe they ordered pizzas at one point, but yes, he did. They were mesmerized," she said.

"And then he disappeared without a trace?"

She smiled and shook her head. "Now, now," she chided gently, "that would be telling. Let me unfold the story in my own way."

That was just like Miss Dorothy, full of mystery and kindness all at the same time, directing things without anyone or anything feeling managed or manipulated. But I'm getting ahead of myself—allow me to make a proper introduction. My name is Robert Berger, Robbie to my friends. And Miss Dorothy was, and is, indeed my friend.

Have you ever had life hand you a moment that was inexplicably perfect? Like having a person, or a set of circumstances, say, show up when you least expected but needed them most?

We almost never have a good explanation for why or how these moments happen, but when they do, we often can't shake the feeling that higher powers are in play. Karma, perhaps? Maybe we're not supposed to understand or question those moments, or view them as a puzzle we have to solve. "Objects in the rearview mirror might be much closer than they appear"—all we have to do is pay attention and look around. Sometimes things just *are*, and we have the choice of whether to notice, believe, and take action . . . or not.

That's how it was when I met Miss Dorothy. The story she told me—the one I'm about to tell you—began many years ago. My role in it came about much more recently.

I've had a somewhat checkered career. There have been times when I was on top of the world, successful and well-regarded. And then there were stretches when circumstances or my own bad choices conspired to bring me down. During these more challenging times I held a wide variety of jobs, in a number of different fields.

One of these was with a company that provided "home assistance to seniors," helping make day-to-day living a bit easier for their elderly clientele. I cleaned windows, organized closets and garages, did the grocery shopping, and assisted in cooking and preparing meals. The money was nothing special, but the work was easy and offered me a particularly rewarding side benefit. I discovered that many of these older folks didn't really order our services to get their homes cleaned or their shopping done. They had us come around simply to sit and talk, or maybe enjoy a nice cup of tea. A house, no matter how big or beautiful, gets lonely fast without children or loved ones around, so I did not mind at all stepping in and offering a little companionship. In fact, that part of the job appealed to me immensely.

Many of our clients had had lives that sounded wonderful—they had owned companies, written books, traveled, parented large, happy families, accomplished amazing things. It often puzzled me how they ended up needing, and wanting, our company's services.

I loved to listen as they recounted episodes from earlier times, their eyes lighting up and voices going soft as they spoke of loved ones and children; the way they giggled with delight or embarrassment about particular events from their youth; the pride in their voices when they revealed some of their greatest accomplishments, none of which was ever easy.

Every story was an adventure, and each person came fully to life as we journeyed through the years. Though I had the feeling some might have added a little color from their own imaginations, the tales were always filled with passion and sincerity. Whenever we landed back in the here-and-now, they were often sad and wistful. No matter how exciting or dramatic their pasts had been, all of my assigned folks seemed to share the same current reality—a sense of loneliness.

For many, there was something else that gnawed on them, like a beaver on a giant tree. Regret!

These individuals peppered our conversations with, "If only I had . . . ," "Why didn't I . . . ," and other expressions of lost opportunity. "I wish I had spent more time with my wife. Now she is gone, and I miss her so much," one said. And another: "Why was I always so angry? Why didn't I just laugh more often?"

I recall an older gentleman who was particularly tormented about his life. More than once he said to me, "I wish I had been a better father. I just never made any time for my kids. They grew up and moved on, and now they have families of their own. Here and there they call to check on me, but I know it's more from obligation than anything else, and I can't blame them. They've just become who I was to them so many years ago. If I could get a second chance to live my life all over again, I would do things so differently."

Often I left their homes feeling great sadness in my heart. Looking back now, though, I realize these folks were teaching me a priceless lesson: the true value and importance of time.

When I was much younger, I read something about time that has stayed with me since. All of us, this article said, have about seventy years in which to create our lives. Start with the average life span, subtract the first few years, when we aren't really conscious of ourselves as even having a life, then subtract the last few years, which are often a time when we have less say in how our lives go. That leaves us with about seventy years—seventy glorious summers—to be who we are going to be.

When we're born we get a birth certificate, which lists an opening date and a location. Other than that, it's a blank piece of paper. It doesn't come with guarantees or promises, nor does it give advice or offer an insurance policy. The only thing we know for certain is that whether we have seventy, or even eighty or ninety summers, eventually they will run out, and a different certificate will list our closing date.

So the message from my clients was clear. We should never lose sight of the fact that time is a gift, and the only thing we really can't get back in life. It's the ultimate investment, holding more value than any currency, rank, or title, and once it's gone, it's gone.

The days I spent with these older folks prompted some long-overdue self-examination. How did I really want to spend my time, and with whom? Just as importantly, how would I rather not spend my time? What would actually living true to myself be like?

When we are seventy years old and look in the mirror, we can complain all we want and invoke all the excuses in the world as to why our lives turned out as they did. But we won't be able to ignore the fact that the reflection looking back at us is of the person responsible.

My experiences reminded me of a quote that a friend of mine told me, from a poem written by composer and writer Dale Wimbrow in 1934, called "The Guy in the Glass":

> You can fool the whole world down the pathway of years
> And get pats on the back as you pass,
> But your final reward will be heartaches and tears
> If you've cheated the guy in the glass.

I started to wonder if I had been cheating myself, and what I might be able to do about that. The stage was set for the meeting that would change my life.

CHAPTER ONE

Miss Dorothy

Just like any Monday morning, I strolled into the head office to pick up my schedule with the names and addresses of clients I would see that week. I had no way of knowing this Monday would be different from all the rest and would set my life on a completely different course. I noticed a new name on the schedule, with the notation that she preferred to be called by her first name, Dorothy, along with the address and to-do list. I scanned through the items. Nothing major—shopping, helping around the house, and chaperoning her on walks through the park. It looked like an easy assignment. She had contracted for a two-hour visit, five days a week. "A well-to-do lady," I thought, because though our caregiver wages were fairly low, the company's services were not cheap.

When I parked my Volkswagen Beetle in front of her house later that morning, my first thought was that I was at the wrong place, and I checked the address again to make sure. The home was huge, a three-story, red brick structure designed in the style of an old English farmhouse. The steep roof, layered with orange clay shingles, and the white-painted window frames contrasted perfectly with the brick. Hanging baskets on the front windows overflowed with colorful blooming plants.

The enormous house sat on a much larger piece of land. A formal front garden was carefully laid out with rows of abundantly blossoming annuals and perennials, including what must have been hundreds of roses creating an almost overwhelming, lovely aroma. The garden was surrounded by a neatly trimmed, emerald lawn that looked soft and lush.

The place was impeccably kept, manicured down to the finest detail. Not the kind of home I was used to seeing on my visits. This one looked more like a small castle, a mansion belonging to someone rich and famous. I revised my previous assumption that this would be an easy gig, thinking to myself, "If I have to clean all those windows—good luck! I'm going to have my work cut out for me."

I strode quickly up the walk to the imposing stoop and yanked the chain hanging to the right of the oversized, antique double front doors. I could hear a chime inside the house, but the chain was also connected to a large, weathered bell over the front doors that looked like it might have once served on an old schooner. It rang loudly and wildly, interrupting the peaceful quietness, and I wished I hadn't pulled so hard. "Shush!" I thought, "Quiet down, already!"

A few seconds later, I heard a faint female voice from inside telling me to enter, so I reached for one of the giant silver door rings and pushed. As the door swung open, I gaped in amazement. The interior of the home was no less impressive than the outside. In the center of a blinding white marble foyer was a massive, antique mahogany table inlaid with mosaic tiles. A tall, expensive-looking ceramic vase on the table held an arrangement of exquisite fresh flowers that filled the entrance hall with the happy scent of spring.

The effect was stunning and reminded me more of the lobby of a luxury hotel than a place where someone actually lived. I looked down at my beat-up work shoes, wondering if I should remove them, but then remembered my socks were in worse shape than the shoes. I felt very much out of place.

"Come in, please, and close the door," I heard the same voice say, and then I saw her for the very first time. She looked every bit like the home she lived in, dressed in an exquisitely tailored, cream-colored suit, perfectly matching shoes with tiny heels, and tasteful pearl earrings. Her pure-white hair was coiffed into a tidy bun. She moved with a sort of graceful formality that reminded me of the Queen of England at an official diplomatic gathering. I couldn't possibly have guessed her age—maybe in her eighties, but it was clear the actual number of her years did not matter in this person's life. She carried herself like a much younger woman, exuding charm, style, discipline, and great elegance. Her tone of voice was soft and kind yet had a firm undertone that suggested strength and determination.

The sparkle in her eyes and spring in her step led me to believe there was even more to her than met the eye. I sensed she did not need any kind of help, and I was a bit confused as to why she had ordered our services at all. I also had a strong hunch she was the designer of that spectacular garden out front, and probably was herself the gardener who brought all that beauty to life. She glided over, greeting me in such a friendly and familiar way that one would have thought we had known each other for years.

"You must be Robert," she said, clasping my hand warmly and looking me straight in the eye.

"Yes, ma'am," I replied. "Robbie."

"Ah, none of this 'ma'am' stuff. Call me Dorothy," she said. "I'm delighted to meet you, Robbie."

"Nice to meet you, too, ma' . . . , eh, Miss Dorothy," I replied, not quite able to bring myself to drop the "Miss."

"Come on in," she said, leading the way into a sitting room. "May I offer you a cup of tea? Maybe a little snack, sandwiches? Are you hungry?"

Had I heard correctly? Did she just offer me tea? I thought that was why *I* was there—to help *her*.

"No, thank you, Miss Dorothy," I declined politely, "but thank you for offering."

"Well, your loss. I just brewed an amazing pot of wild orange blossom tea with rose petal extract. I like to sweeten it slightly with a touch of rare organic Hawaiian honey. I'll bring two cups in case you change your mind. Make yourself comfortable. I'll be right back." She disappeared through a side door.

Who *was* this lady? I sat there baffled, not knowing what to think. After a moment, I began to look around the room, taking it all in. Like the foyer, it was a wonder, further confirmation of the magnificence of the home. The seating consisted of soft beige leather chairs and a leather sofa, arranged around a substantial teak coffee table. The décor communicated warmth, elegance, and comfort, but it was decidedly sophisticated and contemporary. I would have expected a more traditional, "grandmotherly" look. "Pretty hip grandma," I thought.

Behind the sofa, dark blue damask draperies were drawn back to reveal a bank of floor-to-ceiling windows and French doors that overlooked the true jewel of the house—a magnificent, park-like backyard. It was extensive and picture-postcard-perfect, with more beautiful gardens giving way to groomed, wooded pathways. I stared at the expansive landscape in disbelief.

Turning back to the interior, I noticed for the first time that the sitting room had a theme. The walls were adorned with a number of realistically detailed oil paintings of owls. Tastefully framed photographs and other artifacts of the majestic birds were arranged on side tables and shelves. The centerpiece was an enormous portrait over the fireplace of a fierce-looking, brown-and-black owl with bright, orange eyes.

Staring into those eyes, I was jolted by a flood of long-forgotten memories. As a boy I spent many summers and holidays on my grandparents' farm. Theirs wasn't a small, mom-and-pop operation, mind you, but a fairly sizable commercial enterprise. Down the road from the large farmhouse, a complex of four barns, each the size of a supertanker, housed more than 40,000 chickens and 25,000 rabbits that roamed freely in enormous, surrounding pens. A collection of ducks, geese, horses, dogs, cats, and even a peacock named Hugo rounded out the menagerie.

In front of the farmhouse was a manmade lake of several acres my grandfather had dug out himself with a bulldozer. Over time nature settled in, filling the hole with water and covering the banks with reeds and plentiful wildflowers. It was by no means a manicured koi pond, but rather what you would expect on a large farm: a natural-looking reservoir with all the accompanying flora and fauna.

Grandfather stocked it with trout and carp and built a small pier. We kids loved it, especially in the summer when we went swimming, pushing each other off inner tubes and jumping from the little dock into the lake's refreshing, chilly depths.

One warm summer evening when I was about eleven, I grabbed a fishing rod from the boat shed and positioned myself on the end of the pier, dipping my toes into the cool water. The disappearing light bathed the countryside in a pastel glow, and a warm breeze gently rippled the lake's surface.

I could hear pond grass rustling at the water's edge and a few birds singing. Faint sounds drifted from the kitchen as my grandmother prepared dinner, and I knew my grandfather would soon be walking up the hill from the barns after finishing the day's chores. All was calm, peaceful, and idyllic.

I made a short cast and absentmindedly reeled in the line a few feet. After several minutes of staring into the quiet dusk, daydreaming, I began to have the unmistakable, spine-tingling sensation you get when you feel you are being watched. Slowly I turned my head to look over my left shoulder.

And there it was. Perched atop one of the pier's wooden posts, no more than ten feet away, sat a huge owl. I hadn't heard it land. The farm was surrounded by forests and undeveloped property, so I had seen owls before, sitting in trees or flying by in the distance, and I had heard their hooting calls in the night. But I would never have imagined one would come so close to humans.

Certainly memory tends to warp our recollection of things sometimes, like a funhouse mirror, making them larger, more dramatic, or more intense in our stories than they probably really were. But from the point of view of an eleven-year-old, the bird looked enormous, and I was terrified.

I snapped my head back around and squeezed my eyes shut, as if to deny what I thought I had just seen. Otherwise, I kept perfectly still. Then, taking a deep breath, I turned my head again, ever so slowly. The owl was still sitting there, staring at me intently. During this second look, I felt less frightened and began to notice how beautiful it was, sleek feathers marbled in brown, black, pale gray, and creamy white, with ear tufts standing up like horns. The most captivating feature, though, were the glowing orange eyes. The creature and I locked gazes for what seemed like an eternity but must have been only a second or two. Time and place seemed to disappear, and I felt it was staring me down with simultaneous interest and indifference. An instant later the owl spread its powerful wings and lifted gracefully into the air. I watched it fly off and sat transfixed for a few minutes, trying to process what had just happened, before packing up the gear and heading toward the house. I hadn't thought about all this in years and was caught off guard by the overwhelming nostalgia and emotion that washed over me as I looked into the eyes of the owl in the portrait.

The return of Miss Dorothy with a tea cart interrupted my reverie. We sat on the sofa, she poured, and the tea was indeed something else. I had never tasted anything so aromatic—full-flavored, with a mild hint of orange and just enough sweetness. Even more delightful was the array of scones, tarts, and other baked goods she set out, all of which, of course, she had made herself. That first day we just sipped, ate, and talked for two hours about everything and nothing.

Yes, I decided, there was something very different about Miss Dorothy. She was a puzzle, but I could tell she was a special lady, and I liked her from the moment I met her.

The next day she handed me a shopping list with only three items on it—milk, bread, and butter. I was fairly certain her refrigerator and cupboard were well-stocked and that she could easily get to the market herself, but of course I did not question her request. I figured she had her reasons and maybe even wanted me to feel that my services were indeed needed. I returned with the groceries in fewer than twenty minutes. Walking back into the house, I could already smell the tea and goodies fresh from the oven.

As we settled into the sitting room, I asked what else I could help her with. She smiled and said that was all for today and we should just enjoy our tea. Her desire for me to simply sit and visit wasn't unusual in my job, as I've mentioned. I was accustomed to providing company as well as household help to the often lonely seniors who were our clients. It was part of the job and something I not only didn't mind but generally enjoyed. What surprised me about Miss Dorothy was that she did not give the impression she was the least bit lonely or sad. She laughed and smiled easily and always seemed to be in the best of moods. In fact, I don't believe I have ever seen her upset or frustrated. She clearly loved her life, seeming to embrace and enjoy every minute, far more than many people I knew in their twenties and thirties.

But what I came to admire most was that Miss Dorothy was the genuine article. Her way of being wasn't an act; she had no interest in impressing me or anyone else. She was who she was. To me she was one of the most amazing human beings I had ever known.

You can probably tell I grew fonder of her with every visit, and not because she gave me less to do than I had expected. I would have done anything for her, even detailed all those windows on the front of her house—which, by the way, she never once asked me to wash in the two years she was a client. She didn't explain, and I didn't ask, who actually cleaned her house and cared for her garden. Maybe she did some of the work herself, but I suspect there must have been a small army of people tasked with keeping her home and grounds impeccable at all times. I did help with a few little things, but mainly we just talked as we sat, drank tea, and enjoyed each other's company.

She was a marvelous storyteller, and her tales took me back to the time in my childhood when I first discovered, with wonder, my own ability to bring a story to life because my imagination made it so. She shared a few things about her past and her travels but never really revealed much about herself. Mostly she encouraged me to talk about *my* life, which I did almost in spite of myself. She maintained a sense of mystery, as if there was something important she was not telling me.

All that changed one afternoon when I had been visiting Miss Dorothy for about a month. She began relating a story that day of unimaginable, some would say improbable, events she purported to be factual. At the time, however, and in all the time since, I have never questioned her words. I knew they were spoken in truth—I saw it in her eyes.

We were again relaxing comfortably in the sitting room, enjoying tea and baked miracles, when she leaned back into the sofa and sighed deeply. "Beautiful," she said softly. "Isn't he the most handsome and perfect creature you ever laid eyes on?"

It took me a second to realize she was referring to the oil portrait of the majestic-looking owl.

"Ah, yes indeed," I replied. "It's quite a painting."

"Oh," she said, shaking her head. "This is so much more than a painting." Then she turned to me with great curiosity and excitement. "Robbie, what do you know about owls?"

"Well, not much," I said. "I think they are absolutely beautiful, almost mystical in appearance. I got very close to one once when I was a boy. I'd forgotten all about it until the first day I came here. Your painting sparked my memory." And I told her what had taken place at the lake on my grandparents' farm.

"Lucky you," she said, when I had finished the story. "My friend Robbie, sounds like you had a very special visitor."

It was the first time she had called me her friend.

"You see, owls don't just drop in on people. They have no desire to frighten us," she said. "Rather, they are respectful of our time and space. They understand the human world better than we do, but they generally prefer not to interfere. So when owls choose to come close, it's not because they are curious. Their visits have much greater purpose and meaning than that."

I was completely at a loss and sat there with my mouth open.

"How much time do you have?" she asked suddenly.

I looked at my watch and told her I had to leave in about an hour.

"Not just today," she replied with a smile. "I mean over the next few weeks."

I had already changed my schedule to see her at the end of the day, so that it wouldn't matter if I stayed longer than the allotted two hours. My visits were always much longer, but of course I never said anything about this to the office. They would have charged her more for my extra time, and I couldn't have that.

"Oh . . . ummm," I stammered. "Well, as much time as you like."

"Good," she said. "We will need it. There is much I have to share with you, and we had better get started. See you tomorrow."

The next day I arrived for our scheduled meeting as usual at 3:00 p.m. sharp. I hadn't rung the annoying bell since the first day and simply entered the unlocked front door, as Miss Dorothy had instructed me, as if it were my own house.

Stepping into the foyer, I immediately sensed something wasn't quite right, and it took me a few seconds to realize what it was. The usual welcoming aroma was missing. No tea? No pastries?

How quickly we leap to conclusions the instant something seems to be just a little bit off! More often than not we envision a worst-case scenario. My first thought was that Miss Dorothy might be ill or, God forbid, might have fallen and was lying hurt somewhere in the house.

I called her name urgently, my voice coming out as more of an alarmed shout than I intended. She charged out of the sitting room with her index finger to her lips, signaling me to keep quiet. With the other hand, she motioned that I should follow, and I tiptoed after her, trying not to make any noise.

The draperies in the sitting room were drawn almost closed, allowing in only a sliver of sunlight. I could feel a slight breeze of fresh air circulating through the room and realized the French doors leading to the terrace and back garden were ajar. In all the weeks I had been visiting with Miss Dorothy in this room, those doors had never been open. In fact, she had shown me around the first floor of the house when I began my assignment, but the tour did not include the upstairs or the backyard. She never explained or even mentioned the garden and lovely woods behind it, but I had the feeling they were very special to her.

I paused to let my eyes adjust to the dim light, intending to drop my backpack into the large chair next to the sofa, as I always did. When outlines of the furniture came into focus, I walked slowly into the room and then froze. Sitting on the chair back, less than an arm's length away, was a large owl with glowing orange eyes.

"Come," Miss Dorothy said, taking me by the hand and squeezing gently. "I want you to meet someone. Her name is Fabella."

Though I've often tried to recall what I thought or how I felt at that very moment, I can't remember a thing. I was dumbstruck and completely unable to move.

"Fabella," Miss Dorothy said softly. "This is Robbie."

The owl tilted her head slightly to one side and looked directly into my eyes.

"Robbie, you may touch her," Miss Dorothy murmured.

Though the size of the bird intimidated me, she seemed calm and gentle. Her feathers looked soft, and the two furry horns above the eyes gave her a sense of majesty.

"Touch her," I heard Miss Dorothy say again from behind me. "She will not hurt you; she is very loving and wanted to meet you."

I lifted my hand and ever so slowly extended it towards the owl. When I was within a few inches, she leaned forward and met my fingers halfway, allowing me to stroke the feathers on her neck, which were like velvet.

Nothing could have prepared me for what happened next. I started to pull my hand back but within a split second she had shifted position to perch on my forearm. As I raised her up a bit higher and closer to my chest for stability, she suddenly moved toward me and rubbed the side of her large head against my left cheek. My mind went into overdrive, and I realized I was experiencing one of the most amazing moments in my life. She was absolutely beautiful, and I was totally in love with owls.

"Does she live here?" I whispered, barely breathing.

"She chooses my garden as her home, but that's entirely up to her. She can live wherever she likes. Once in a while she comes near to say hello and check on me, as we have a very personal connection. But she is free as the wind."

I eased into the leather chair, holding my arm steady. Fabella stepped off my forearm and settled onto the armrest, while Miss

Dorothy nestled into the sofa, looking at me and the owl with complete contentment.

After a few seconds of silence she said, "What I'm about to tell you took place years ago. Very few people knew about it until just recently, when a man named Dalton—whom no one had ever seen before—crashed a senior executive meeting at a company called Hoppe Enterprises."

And so she began to tell me her story.

CHAPTER TWO

A Tempest in the Conference Room

Saturday, 6:50 a.m.

The elevator doors parted smoothly, allowing eight similarly dressed business executives to exit. Though it wasn't technically a workday, they all wore formal corporate attire—conservative suits, traditional ties and scarves, wingtips, and pumps—no business casual here. The unmotivated cluster shuffled glumly down a long hallway toward an oversized, frosted-glass door bearing the etched inscription, Innovation Room.

The executive conference room was on the twenty-eighth floor of the Hoppe Enterprises corporate headquarters building. Floor-to-ceiling glass windows provided a spectacular view of the downtown skyline, the river wending its way through the city, and a municipal park that was slowly coming to life with joggers and people walking their dogs.

As they waited, a few members of the senior management team looked longingly out the windows, wishing they could trade their places in the glass prison for a bit of Saturday morning freedom. The day, they knew, would be a long one. The dark, polished walnut surface of the enormous conference table reflected worried faces as they slowly took their seats in the high-backed, black leather chairs. The company was in trouble, and no one knew what was coming next. Once a global business giant and formidable competitor, Hoppe

Enterprises had been losing momentum for quite some time, long before the recent economic crisis. Although profits had remained fairly respectable, the CEO thought otherwise and tormented his leadership team mercilessly to improve the bottom line by slashing expenses, primarily headcount.

Rumors abounded. Would they be taken over? Certain divisions sold? Would there be more layoffs? "Contingency Meeting" read the subject line of the email the executive team had received the day before, just before 5:00 p.m. Weekend plans evaporated as the reality sank in. The message came from CEO Joachim Ulrich, also known as "Old Iron Heart," among the kinder epithets.

Company lore had it that he was born without feelings and very little, if any, soul. Few had seen him smile. He had a small collection of ex-wives, no children, and associates rather than friends. It had puzzled many when, three years ago, the Hoppe board had approved such a tyrant to be CEO. Hoppe had built its fortune on being people-focused and service-driven, and Ulrich was anything but. The company's success had continued for a while as Ulrich squeezed out profits through systematic downsizing and cost-cutting; then the gradual decline had set in.

There was no question but that they would attend this meeting, despite the unreasonable day and hour. When Mr. Ulrich commanded, they had to obey. He was famous for spontaneous, "off with their heads" moments when he fired people on the spot. With the prospect of job loss and career crash a constant threat, they were stuck.

The door swung open and the CEO marched in, flanked by his henchmen, Chief Financial Officer Gerald Klein and Chief Strategy Officer August Lieb. Ulrich was short and heavyset, with a close-cropped beard covering most of his face. His overall appearance gave a textbook impression of "mean"—long, needle nose, eyes black as coal and an ever-present aura of arctic chill. It was impossible to read the man, but his sour expression gave everyone fair warning to stay clear.

He stood at the head of the table and glanced around the room, stone-faced and silent. Then he launched forth. "You all know why you are here. No excuses. I want results, immediate results. You've failed to increase profits, so now you will further decrease expenses. Our labor costs stayed flat in the last quarter, but so did sales. That's not how I run a business. You will cut the labor pool another thirty percent across the board."

Joseph Walt, the senior vice president of operations, looked at him in shock. "That would be devastating. We've already cut our workforce in half over the past two years. Who's going to be left to run the business? Besides, the media would eat us alive. I respectfully request you reconsider and give us an opportunity to complete the plan my team has been working on that doesn't involve more companywide layoffs."

Ulrich turned slowly and fixed Walt with a piercing look. "You are right. There are easier ways to cut costs, like removing ineffective members of senior management. And I'm going to start with you, Walt. You are fired—effective now. Don't bother to clear out your office. Your severance package and belongings will be sent to you."

There were a few gasps, and Ulrich whirled back around, his beady eyes shining. "Would anyone else like to tell me what I should do as the CEO? No? I didn't think so. Next agenda item: I'm bringing in a consultant to make sure you get all this done. He's a turnaround specialist, and between him and me, we will set this company back on track. He'll be here today to get started."

Hardly pausing for breath, he continued, "Mr. Klein, Mr. Lieb, and I must attend to some pressing business over the weekend and will be back in the office Monday morning. By then I expect to see a strategic expense reduction plan with detailed diagnostics and implementation tactics. Do I make myself clear, ladies and gentlemen?"

He didn't wait for an answer before wheeling around and sweeping abruptly out of the conference room with his two sidekicks in tow.

"Well, there goes the weekend," everyone was thinking. Pressing business? What was it this time? A couple of days at his private hunting lodge, or deep-sea fishing on his newly purchased luxury sports boat? They hated him, and now he had trumped their loathing by destroying the last hope Hoppe Enterprises really had—he had fired Joe Walt. Unbelievable.

Walt stood up and looked around the table, but no one met his gaze. A few mumbled an "I'm so sorry, Joe," but most simply stared ahead in silence.

He shook his head and strode to the meeting room door. As he reached for the handle, the door suddenly swung inward and a tall, gray-haired man stuck his head in the doorway.

"Hello!" the stranger said with a grin. "May I come in for a moment?" Without hesitating he ambled into the room, nodding at Walt, who was still standing by the door, and walked over to pause behind Ulrich's chair at the head of the table.

He was well over six feet tall and dressed in an expensive but ill-fitting dark-gray suit, with a worn white shirt and red bow-tie that was a bit askew. In fact, his entire appearance was somehow—off. He carried a rumpled trench coat caked with mud on one sleeve, and his round glasses tilted precariously higher on one side than the other.

"Looks like I've arrived a bit late," he said, smiling at the gloomy faces around the room. "Mr. Walt, please, be seated and continue your meeting."

"You're . . . the consultant?" Walt asked hesitantly.

"Ah, well, yes. I suppose I am a consultant of sorts," the stranger said pleasantly, his eyes twinkling. "I'm here to assess the situation and offer some guidance."

"In that case, you are late," Walt said flatly. "It's not my meeting—I've just been fired. Ulrich has already 'assessed the situation' and given the order to eliminate thousands more positions worldwide. All those people—our people. Some of them have worked for us from day one. It will be devastating for them and their families, not to mention the company. This is not the way to fix problems. It's not who we are!" His voice choked with emotion, and he turned again towards the door.

"Not so fast, Mr. Walt," the consultant called out. "I would like for you to stay a while. I've been given carte blanche to do what's necessary, and at the moment that means continuing to seek your counsel. Please take your seat again."

Confused but curious, Walt returned to his chair. "How did he know my name?" he thought. The consultant dropped his trench coat onto a chair at the back of the room and poured himself a glass of water from the pitcher on the conference table. He moved to the windows and looked down at the park and the river, nodding and chuckling as if recalling something. The men and women in the room remained transfixed. The consultant exuded a powerful, calming energy, and he seemed somehow familiar, at home in this place and with them.

He perched on the edge of the conference table and looked slowly around at each face. "My name is Dalton," he began, "and I'm pleased to make your acquaintance. I'm not here to point out your flaws, or tell you what you have to do to fix the current situation, or convince you what's right or wrong. I can't change you or the way things are, and therefore I will not even try.

"In fact, I'm a firm believer that trying to force change onto anyone yields little or no results. If people don't see the point of the change, the effort is useless. Only you have the power to initiate real, meaningful change in this company and in your lives. My goal is to help you realize you can, that when all is said and done it's your own belief and willpower that will bring about buy-in for the change you want to cause, which will create the future you all desire."

He paused and pursed his lips, stroking his chin. "Now as to the consulting," he continued. "You see, the way I, uh, consult, is by telling stories. So let me share one with you. It's about a boy, and it happened a long time ago, though it seems like yesterday."

CHAPTER THREE

Keg's Story

It was raining. Keagen could hear it drumming on the roof through the haze of his early morning half-sleep. He would get wet riding his bike to school, and probably be late at that. And in trouble again.

He dragged himself out of bed and over to the window, pressing his nose to the chilled glass and looking down into the street below. The view outside was gray, as it always seemed to Keagen, even when it wasn't raining. He opened the window a crack and let the cool air finish waking him up.

At the little neighborhood market on the corner, Mr. Gillespie, clad in a black slicker, was stacking produce onto the weathered wooden stands tucked under rust-stained awnings on either side of the shop door. The squash, tomatoes, apples, heads of lettuce, even the shiny mackerel, all seemed covered in a dull film, reflecting the slate color of the sky.

A sudden gust of wind sent the rain pelting down harder than ever, splashing on the street pavers and swelling the puddle at the corner storm drain into a small lake in a matter of seconds. The rickety street sign creaked and wavered, making its faded letters even more difficult to read: Sledge Lane. "Sludge Lane," as the perpetually overworked, underpaid residents sometimes wryly referred to it, only partly in jest.

Keagen pushed the window shut and rested his head on the sill. He really didn't want to go to school, especially not today. He turned back toward the bed. Just a few more minutes . . .

Downstairs his mother began her singsong ritual. "Keagen!" she called wearily. "Get up. Come to breakfast. School starts in forty-five minutes." His sister had already caught a ride to school with friends, and his father had left for the office two hours ago, as usual.

Glancing reluctantly at his bed, Keagen pulled on his clothes, made a pass at his teeth with the toothbrush and lumbered down the steps into the kitchen. He was tall for his twelve years and chubby, a gentle bear of a boy with a shock of unruly blond hair that persisted in falling into his light-blue eyes.

"Did you do your homework last night?" his mother asked. The dialog was always the same.

"Yes."

"Don't forget your books."

"Ok."

"Take your rain jacket."

"Uh-huh."

Keagen finished his cereal and headed out the door. He wheeled his bicycle from the garage, tugging the hood of his parka over his head and throwing his book bag into the front basket.

The school was only about two miles away, and he actually loved the ride, but he wasn't fond of the rain. He zipped out into the street, pedaling through his neighborhood and turning onto the divided road that paralleled the forest and river at the edge of the village.

The rain stung his face, and his wet sneakers slipped off the pedals. At the top of the steep, curving hill that marked the homestretch on the way to the school, he paused. Taking this hill on sunny days, he sometimes imagined his bike was a sailboat, a graceful sloop like the ones he had read about, like the model of the racing yacht he had built that held a place of honor on a shelf in his bedroom.

He was captaining her around the world solo. *"What a remarkable feat!"* the media would cry. *"And he's only twelve? How did he become such an accomplished sailor? He doesn't live anywhere near an ocean! His parents must be so proud. The weather today—such a challenge!"*

"No problem at all," Captain Keagen tells them boldly, *"It's just a nor'easter; I'm used to 'em, nothing to worry about."*

A truck rumbled in the road behind him, startling Keagen out of his daydream. "Late," he thought, "Late, late, *late*." He shoved off on his bike at full speed down the hill. At the halfway point, something moving at the edge of the woods to the right caught his eye. A small, gray, tiger-striped kitten stumbled to the edge of the pavement, shivering in the rain.

Poor little guy, Keagen thought. He's lost from his mom, and cold, and hungry. The next instant he found himself somersaulting in midair. Distracted by the kitten, he'd steered right into a rain-filled pothole. Boy and bike went over nose first, with Keagen landing hard on his bottom and skidding to a stop.

The spill knocked the wind out of him, and he lay on the ground for a bit to get his breath back, shaking his head to clear it. His hands were scraped, but he could tell he wasn't hurt badly. Scrambling to his feet, he felt an odd sensation on his backside—cold air. His almost-new black jeans were splattered with mud. As he reached around to his buttocks, he shut his eyes in horror. The entire seat of his pants was ripped to shreds, and his underwear was not in much better shape.

"This can't be happening," he thought. "Not today, of all days." There was no time to ride back to his house, change pants and ride all the way to school again. Besides, his mother would still be at home. She didn't leave for her part-time job until noon. He would have to explain, then get a lecture about being careless and costing them money they didn't have.

But he couldn't go into the school, into class, with his bare buttocks exposed, either. It was hard enough to fly under the radar and out of range of the cluster of bullies who terrorized the odd and the meek in his grade. They would fall on him like a pack of hungry wolves. Then there would be the snickers, the pointing, and the whispers from the other kids. No, it was out of the question. But so was playing hooky. If he just didn't show up, the school would call his mother, who would send out a search party. His immediate future was looking dimmer by the minute.

Then he had a flash of inspiration—Bert! He would stop by his friend's auto repair shop. It was barely a block from the school. Surely Bert would have something Keagen could use to patch his britches. He picked up the bike—undamaged, save for a few scratches—and scanned the roadside. The kitten was nowhere in sight.

He pedaled the rest of the way down the hill as fast as he dared, given the fragile condition of his pants, making a sharp left before he reached the school to avoid being seen. He took a slightly roundabout route to the rambling wooden building that housed Bert's Autowerx and rode directly into one of the two open bays.

"Bert!" he shouted to the small, wiry man who peered around the open hood of a black sedan. "Bert, you've got to help me."

"Well, hello there, Keg." Bert used the nickname Keagen had been called by family and friends, with the exception of his mother and father, for as long as he could remember. As Keagen approached adolescence and grew taller and rounder, the affectionate moniker had become something of a liability.

"What's the problem?" Bert asked, wiping grease from his hands with an oily rag.

Keagen turned around and displayed the damage. "I fell off my bike, and I'm late for school," he blurted. "Do you have anything to fix this?"

"That's quite a hole. You sure you're all right?" Bert asked. Keagen nodded. "Well, ok. Hmmm, let's see. Got some tire patches, but they probably wouldn't stick to cloth," Bert mused. "We might be able to make something out of those tarps over in the corner."

"Wrong color," Keagen said flatly, staring at the pile of beige tarpaulins. Then he brightened. Rushing over to a large bin next to a tire rack, Keagen rummaged through and pulled out two pieces of thin black metal. "What about these?"

"Those are scrap, and you're welcome to 'em, but how on earth are you going to hitch those to your pants?"

"You could punch a couple of holes and I'll tie them to my belt, from inside my jeans," Keagen offered. "We can cut away the torn parts, and then all that will show is the black metal."

"Yeah, but Keg, how are you gonna sit, or even walk, much less ride?"

"Bert, *please*! I don't have much time," Keagen pleaded.

Within a few minutes, the makeshift industrial patches were in place. Keagen gingerly eased himself back onto his bicycle and pedaled away in the rain, with Bert giving a cheery thumbs-up.

As Keagen rode toward the school building, the metal pieces banged and scraped against each other, threatening to work their way out of his pants, but the rigging held.

He parked his bike, grabbed his book bag and headed for his first class, math with Mr. Heldrich. He was twenty minutes late.

Bracing himself, he opened the classroom door. Mr. Heldrich stopped mid-sentence and glared. "Mr. Keagen, so good of you to finally grace us with your presence," he droned in his nasal monotone. Keagen noticed he was wearing the same tired brown suit he wore every day. Since this was Tuesday, the suit was accompanied, as usual, by a washed-out green shirt and too-wide orange tie.

"Mr. Keagen, this may be a new record for your tardiness," the teacher continued, absentmindedly smoothing the thin strands of his combed-over hair. "You will, most certainly, be late for your own funeral. But long before that, your lack of interest and limited ability in academics will have made a shambles of your life. You are destined to become a ward of the state. We will all be paying for your upkeep with our tax dollars."

The students, at first riveted by the mini-drama of Keagen's late entrance and the teacher's verbal attack, now were losing interest and began to shift in their seats, whispering among themselves. One or two put their heads on their desks and began to snooze.

Keagen tried not to draw further attention as he moved toward his desk, avoiding eye contact with everyone. It was bad enough being made fun of in front of his classmates, but this particular class included Cassandra McIntosh, the girl of his dreams.

He'd had a crush on her since third grade but never got up the nerve to speak to her. She was tall and slender, with curly golden hair that reached halfway down her back and big, beautiful brown eyes that always seemed warm and kind. Her cute little button nose was sprinkled with tiny freckles . . . and then there were the dimples when she smiled. A while back—as if he would ever forget the exact location, date, hour, minute, and second it happened—she passed him in the hall and actually gave him a look and a smile.

She may as well have been the Medusa from Greek mythology, because when she gazed into his eyes, Keagen turned to stone. Well, almost stone, because the next thing he remembered was slamming his face into an oncoming wall that he could have sworn was not there the day before. He tucked the smile away deep in his heart and had no hopes of ever getting a second one.

And why would he? What would a smart, gorgeous, popular girl like Cassandra ever see in him? He was just average—no, not even average. He was Keagen The Loser!

He had almost reached the safety of his desk when he heard words that struck terror.

"Mr. Keagen, you missed this morning's pop quiz and so have a zero," Mr. Heldrich intoned, "which is a perfect complement to the F you received on your test last Friday. Let's try to catch you up to the rest of the class, shall we? Go to the board and work out the problem there."

"Oh, no," Keagen thought in a panic. "I'm done for." He sidled around the edge of the classroom with his back to the wall. At the last possible moment, he picked up the chalk and faced the board. No one, including Mr. Heldrich, was paying much attention. Keagen breathed a sigh of relief and tried to concentrate on the equations in front of him.

Suddenly he heard a snort, as if someone were choking and laughing at the same time. He glanced over his shoulder. It was Franco, ringleader of the bully kids, sprawled in his front-row seat. "Hey!" he shouted. "What's that on your butt? Have you got some kind of metal thing on your butt?"

Keagen whirled, slamming his back against the blackboard, his face the color of the chalk. The force of the blow pulled loose the twine tying one of the metal plates to his belt. It slipped from his pants and clanged to the floor. The class erupted in shrieks of laughter.

"Metal butt!" screamed Franco. "Keg-o's got a metal butt!" His chief lieutenants, Spike, Bruno, and Katrun, took up the chant and soon the whole class was shouting, "Metal butt!"

Mr. Heldrich stormed to the front of the room. "Turn around!" he ordered. The boy stood frozen. "I said, turn around."

Keagen stepped away from the blackboard and pivoted slowly until his backside was exposed to the class, his torn jeans framing the one remaining metal plate side-by-side with his slightly pink, bare buttock.

The din in the classroom had become deafening. Two of the other teachers, alarmed by the commotion, had come running from their rooms to investigate the cause. Mr. Heldrich's face was beet red. "Quiet!" he shouted at the students. He leveled a menacing gaze at Keagen and said, "To the office. *Now.*"

The rest of the day was even more humiliating than Keagen had feared. After explaining the torn pants to Mr. Heldrich and the principal, he was marched to the boys' locker room to exchange the shredded jeans for a pair of gym shorts. Hoots, catcalls, and an endless stream of laughter followed him up and down the halls and into each classroom.

At lunch, his best friends, Waldo, Gina, and DiDi, shared their sandwiches behind a clump of bushes at the back of the school to spare Keagen the indignity of having to parade through the lunchroom, where Franco would have a captive audience for his taunts.

Waldo was as small as Keagen was large, a short, thin boy given to wearing trousers that were too short and tee-shirts that were too long, adding to his diminutive appearance. Gina was easily as tall as Keagen and even skinnier than Waldo, with round glasses and below-the-shoulders, rather stringy dark hair that she sometimes wore in braids.

DiDi was Keagen's best friend and towered over the other three. He wore glasses that were too big for his face and looked as if he had grown too quickly into his frame. The thinker of the group, Didi contemplated every situation carefully, often getting lost in his thoughts. He was the one they turned to for advice and counsel. And he was loyal to his friends, especially Keagen, to a fault.

All four were on the outer fringes in terms of class popularity and acceptance, but while Waldo and Gina were both smart, DiDi was acknowledged by fellow students and teachers alike to border on genius. Keagen, on the other hand, considered himself to be an average student at best and often wondered why they chose to be his friends.

Mercifully, the first afternoon class was art, taught by Mrs. Stockton. She was a short, pleasant-looking woman in her late fifties, with kind eyes and a round body. Art was Keagen's favorite class, an oasis in the school day where he knew he could relax, partly because Franco & Co. had chosen to take "shop" during this period and so weren't around, and partly because Mrs. Stockton's manner of teaching was remarkably free of judgment and criticism.

Under her gentle guidance, Keagen's imagination knew no bounds, whether he was learning about the color palette or sculpting in clay. Although he wasn't much of a painter, he had considerable talent for sketching. A piece of paper and a pencil were his gateway to undiscovered worlds, where he could be far more than average.

To Violet Stockton's way of thinking, every student—regardless of artistic ability—was brimming with creative potential, a position that often put her at odds with her fellow teachers. News of the "metal butt incident" in Mr. Heldrich's classroom had been the talk of the faculty lounge throughout the day, and Mrs. Stockton found herself defending Keagen's antics.

"That ridiculous boy!" Mr. Heldrich had fumed over his second cup of coffee in the lounge that morning. "He spends most of every class staring out the window. Just when you've started to wonder if he's even all *there* upstairs, he pulls a crazy stunt like this. It's hard enough to crack open their little heads and pour in the math without distractions from weirdos like Keagen."

"You're just jealous because he was able to command more attention from the front of the room than you were, Henry," Mrs. Stockton said acidly. "Seems Keagen came up with a pretty innovative solution to a problem, if you ask me."

"And no one is asking you, Vi," Mr. Heldrich retorted. "We all wish we could supervise 'play time' as you do rather than attempt to teach important educational principles to unwilling hooligans!"

Mrs. Stockton grinned and raised her coffee mug in a salute as the math teacher swept past her in a fury and headed to his next class.

For Keagen, the serenity of art class was followed by the ultimate torment, physical education. It was "Fitness Assessment Day," the event Keagen had been dreading since the school year started. The students were put through a series of timed and measured physical challenges, from the number of sit-ups and pull-ups that could be completed in one minute to dashes, relays, and distance running. The results sentenced each student to a particular unofficial category within his or her grade, ranging, as might be expected, from most to least athletic.

Members of the junior and senior varsity football, basketball, and baseball teams were, of course, at the top of the ladder for the boys, and the cheerleaders, volleyball players, and gym squad ranked highest among the girls.

Despite his secret dreams of making the junior varsity baseball team—the tryouts were a few weeks away—Keagen knew, even before the Fitness Assessment Day trials began, that he and Waldo would be in the bottom-most group.

Franco and his gang were merciless, egged on by Coach Willard, the PE instructor, who had no tolerance for the students he described as "softies." Keagen was tripped as he started off in the 50-yard dash, and Waldo was "accidentally" stepped on by a Franco crony as he attempted his sit-ups.

As they lapped the football field in their timed distance running, somehow the sprinklers were turned on so that Keagen, Waldo, DiDi, and a handful of other slower runners were soaked. As his crowning achievement, Franco pushed Keagen into a huge mud puddle that had formed at the corner of the field from the morning rain and finished things off by dumping a bag of the chalk used to line the fields over Keagen's head.

"He looks ready for the fryin' pan!" Franco chortled, as Coach Willard sent Keagen to the showers.

When the bell rang to end the last period of the day, Waldo, DiDi, and Gina met at Keagen's locker, exchanging worried looks.

"Have you seen him?" Waldo asked.

Gina shook her head. "Not since lunch. I heard what happened in your PE class. I had to deal with some of that from Katrun and her little mean squad during the girls' assessments. Do you think he's already gone home?"

"I doubt it," DiDi said. "He's probably somewhere trying to stay clear of Franco and his mob." The three then looked at each other knowingly and at the same time exclaimed, "The Treehouse!"

The Treehouse had been their secret sanctuary since they were much younger. It was hidden away on the quiet side of the village's popular recreation spot, Silver Lake, named for the shimmer the surface gave off when reflecting the last of the day's sunlight. The side of the lake nearest to town was well-groomed and easily accessible, with a big parking lot adjacent to athletic fields, picnic grounds, and a small sandy beach and bathhouse.

The back part of the lake, by contrast, was surrounded by forest and seldom disturbed by anyone.

Thick undergrowth reached down to the water's edge and made walking virtually impossible—except, that is, for the four friends who had discovered a pathway through the woods leading to a hidden lagoon.

A cluster of old trees with massive trunks grew close to the water and stretched their branches out over the quiet pool. Several years before, the children had taken Gina's father into their confidence, sharing the location of their secret gathering spot and asking his help to build a treehouse there for them.

Though he was thrilled about the project, Keagen was secretly jealous of Gina because her dad was so cool and always willing to help; he seemed to love spending time with his daughter. Keagen wished his father would show as much interest in him.

The structure Gina's dad created wasn't actually a treehouse in the strictest sense—just a few planks nailed together across several sturdy branches, not very high off the ground, creating a floor that would support the weight of the four youngsters.

The highlight was a rope swing Gina's father had attached to one of the upper branches. At the bottom end he secured an old rubber tire, perfect for sailing from the wooden platform out over and into the cool, clear water of the lagoon. The group had spent many summers at the Treehouse playing pirates and treasure hunts, cowboys and Indians, and planning wild adventures about which they would then swear each other to secrecy.

It was a magical place and it was their sanctuary, a refuge where they could escape the often harsh realities that are so difficult for twelve-year-old minds to make sense of. The Treehouse bore witness to the transformation of the youngsters' lives, watching as they turned from playful kids into young teenagers.

Waldo, Gina, and DiDi pedaled their bikes from the school to the lake in record time. As they pushed over the last hump of the narrow path, they could see Keagen's bike dashed onto the ground beside the lagoon. He was sitting on the sandy shore, knees drawn up and head buried in his folded arms.

"It's going to be okay, Keg—everybody knows Franco is just a jerk," Waldo offered sympathetically.

"His name is Keagen!" Gina barked. She was always quick to speak up on Keagen's behalf.

"Okay, okay. Sorry, *Keagen*," Waldo replied, looking like a scolded puppy.

"Franco is a bully and a criminal. He belongs in reform school," Gina added indignantly. DiDi, who was wearing a long face and looking very concerned, said nothing.

"Don't!" Keagen blurted, keeping his head down but holding up both hands. "Don't try to make it all better. It's not going to get any better. It's not just Franco . . . it's me. I can't do anything right. I shouldn't even try. They always thought I was weird before, but after today I'm the joke of the whole school. I hate this place, and I hate my life. Just leave me alone!"

He scrambled to his feet and grabbed his bike. The friends noticed both tires were flat—another Franco calling card. Sobbing, Keagen pushed the bike back onto the path and disappeared into the thicket. Gina called out and started to run after him, but DiDi held her back.

"Let him go," he said. "I don't think there's anything we can do to make him feel better right now."

As Keagen pushed his bike up the long, steep slope toward home, it began to rain again, hard. "Perfect," he thought. "Just another perfect end to a perfect day." He had worked himself into a state of utter despair. "I'm the biggest loser in the entire world," he thought miserably. "No wonder my father wishes he could trade me in for a better son—I would, too, if I had a kid as stupid and worthless as me. He's right when he says I'll never amount to anything."

His mental spin-cycle was interrupted when he noticed a large, oddly shaped bag in the middle of the road. It was hard to make out in the heavy rain, so Keagen pulled down the kickstand on his bike and walked, somewhat cautiously, toward the object. He realized as he got closer that it was not a bag, but a large clump of what looked to be feathers. Not feathers, a bird—a big one. An owl.

CHAPTER FOUR

—◦◦◦—

An Unexpected Houseguest

Keagen could see the creature was breathing, but it seemed to be stunned. Its eyes were wide open and fixed in a glassy stare. Without hesitating, he took off his parka and gently laid it over the owl, then scooped the large bird up in his arms. It was heavier than he expected. The owl didn't struggle against him, or even move. Keagen walked back to the bike and laid his bundle carefully in the front basket.

"You're gonna be okay," he told it in his most reassuring, grownup voice. "We'll get you home, and you'll be fine."

He walked bike and bird the rest of the way to his house in silence, absorbed in thoughts of how to get the owl in from the garage and up the stairs to his room without anyone knowing what he was doing.

He visualized the scene he knew he would find at home: his father would be working at the desk in the corner of the living room that he referred to as his "office." Sallie, his older sister, most likely would be talking on the phone and listening to music. His mother would be busy cooking dinner but would make a point of seeing him as he came in.

As he rolled his bike into the garage, Keagen spotted a large cardboard box in a corner. It was filled halfway with papers—probably some of his father's old notes or records, he thought. More importantly, it was just the right size. He carefully pulled out the contents and placed them on the garage floor, carrying the box back to where he'd left the bike. The owl fit perfectly, and Keagen covered the top with his rain jacket.

As he walked past the kitchen and started up the stairs, his mother peered around the doorway.

"You're late," she said flatly. "Where have you been? And what's in that box?"

"Books," Keagen lied cheerfully. "I stopped at the library. Doing some research for a history project."

"Well, hurry and wash up. Dinner is in ten minutes," she sighed, disappearing back into the kitchen. She reappeared in an instant. "Where are your jeans?"

Keagen froze. He had forgotten he was still wearing gym shorts—an extra pair, since the ones he had donned that awful morning were caked with mud and chalk from PE class. His new black jeans lay in tatters in the bottom of his locker.

"Uh, Coach Willard made us stay after school and do extra workouts," he mumbled nervously. "I didn't change back."

"Well, don't forget to bring them home tomorrow."

Keagen raced to his room, locking the door behind him. He lifted the owl from the box and laid it gently in the middle of his bed. It was huge. The bird seemed to be conscious now and was watching him, still not moving.

"First things first. I have to see where you are injured and dry you off," Keagen explained, as he gingerly stretched out first one wing, then the other. The tips reached almost to the head and foot of his bed. He then felt over the soft black-and-brown feathers covering the bird's body, all the way to its pronounced ear tufts, and examined its legs and feet. The owl remained motionless, the large orange eyes following his every move. Finally Keagen took a towel and softly patted it dry.

"Well, I guess you haven't been shot, or attacked by a dog or some other animal," he said, attempting to sound confident. "But I bet you're hungry. What kinds of things do you eat?" He paused, then scrambled to his bookshelf and pulled out an encyclopedia. After a few moments of reading, he looked up at the owl and made a face. "Ooh, you eat live things, like mice and rats. None of that for you tonight. I'll have to see what I can find in our icebox."

He re-read the scientific name for the kind of owl he thought this one was. "Bubo," he said aloud. "That sounds like a pretty good name for you."

He heard his mother calling and slammed the book shut. "I'll be back in just a while, Bubo," he told the bird and headed out the door.

It was another typical night at the dinner table. His father was holding the evening newspaper in front of his face and eating with his other hand, making sound effects to accompany every story he read.

A short, loud snort meant, "That's a little bit funny," while a disapproving "You must be crazy!" or "Who do you think you are?" indicated disgust with statements or promises from public figures, usually politicians or sports coaches. Keagen particularly enjoyed the full-fledged conversations his dad sometimes held with the newspaper.

"Where do you get stupid ideas like that?" he would blurt suddenly, breaking the silence at the table.

Or, "Even I knew that, you blockhead. *How* much money do they pay you?"

Sometimes, "Don't sound so surprised! Anyone could have told you, but you never listen."

When his mother occasionally interrupted the passionate one-siders, his father would lower the newspaper slightly, revealing only his eyes and nose, then resume reading and conversing, as if the family cared what he was saying.

"That baseball coach is ridiculous," he fumed this evening. "Can you believe it? He actually thinks management is going to stand behind him, with the record he's produced. The guy is delirious."

He peered over the paper after he spoke but didn't wait for any reply. The top of his face quickly disappeared again.

Other than his father's monologues, dinner was generally more a function of food than conversation. If a topic did come up, it usually had to do with Keagen—his grades or some other way in which he was failing, or so it seemed to him. A quiet meal, therefore, was in his mind a peaceful one, and Keagen was always grateful for the silence.

Tonight, however, that was not to be the case. Ignoring his father's outbursts at the newspaper, his mother turned to him and said, "Speaking of baseball, we got a letter in the mail from the school."

Keagen froze. "What now?" he thought in a panic.

"It's about tryouts for the baseball team," she said. "They're in about six weeks."

He let out a relieved breath. "Yeah, I heard about them."

"Well, are you going?" she persisted.

"To the tryouts? No, Mom, I wouldn't stand a chance of making the team. I'm not good at baseball."

"Thank God he knows," his sister chimed in.

"Shut up, Sallie," Keagen snapped.

"*You* shut up!"

"Enough, you two. Cut it out," their mother said firmly. Then turning to her husband, she said, "Dear . . . "

There was no response.

"Todd!" she said more sharply.

"Hmm?" Keagen's father put the newspaper to one side and gave her an absentminded look.

"Why don't you take Keagen to the park this week for some baseball practice? Who knows—with a little help on his skills, he might even be able to make the team."

Keagen's ears perked up. He would have loved to play ball with his dad, anytime, but in the past, whenever he had asked, his father had given him a lecture. It always had something to do with "the real world" or the "importance of responsibility and discipline," and that "food doesn't just magically appear on the table."

He never really understood what his father was talking about. All it meant to him was that his dad had more important things to do than play ball with him. After a while, Keagen stopped asking altogether.

"This week?" his father was saying. "Did you not hear anything I said earlier? We are in the middle of a company restructuring. I'm going to have to work late again every night this week to supervise production, because there's nobody else to do it. And besides, Keagen doesn't even like baseball."

Keagen could feel the familiar frustration welling up inside him. He was sick and tired of people—his own family!—talking about him as if he weren't even there, making comments and assumptions about what he felt and thought. They treated him as if he were invisible.

He was angry, but he said nothing. "Yes, I *do* like baseball," he thought. "But how would you know whether I like it or not? You've never even asked me."

"You heard him," his father went on. "He's not good at baseball, and he wouldn't make the team anyway. He has no chance against those other kids. They are stronger, faster, and more athletically built. Keagen just isn't meant for sports, and a little practice in the park isn't going to change the facts." His dad's face disappeared again behind the newspaper, signaling the end of the discussion on baseball.

Keagen's mother glared at the newspaper with disgust and continued, "Well, I'm sure there are other activities at school that you could sign up for."

"Oh, there *are*," Sallie smirked, with a giggle. "He could be one of those cool kids in the Art Club. Or, I hear they're still looking for people to be in the ballet chorus of the school musical. I would pay money to see my brother in a pink tutu." She proceeded to cackle uncontrollably.

The next thing Sallie knew she was dripping wet from the head down with milk.

"Mom! Dad!" she screamed. "Look what Keagen did to me!"

Their father peered around the side of his newspaper and shouted, "What in the world? Keagen, have you lost your mind? What's the matter with you? Up to your room right now, young man, and consider yourself grounded!"

"But, but, she started it!" Keagen blurted, trying lamely to defend himself.

"One more word, and I get my belt from the closet," came the reply.

Keagen stood up angrily and turned to leave the dining room. Sallie, wiping off the milk with her napkin, gave him a wicked "Gotcha!" smile.

"Take your plate to the kitchen," his mother said.

As he set his dinner dishes in the kitchen sink, Keagen remembered the owl. Retrieving his plate and knife, he opened the refrigerator door and surreptitiously sliced a generous piece of his mother's leftover roast beef, tossed it onto the plate and headed quickly upstairs to his room.

The owl had not moved an inch. It was still lying in the middle of his bed, watching him as he entered.

"Here's your dinner," Keagen said, setting the plate of beef in front of the bird.

He curled up at the foot of his bed and reached out to touch the soft feathers on the owl's chest.

"How was *my* dinner? Well, Bubo, thank you for asking," Keagen said, pretending to have a conversation with the bird. "You know, the usual, nothing out of the ordinary. My dad told me I'm lousy at baseball and sports, like I am at everything else. My sister and I got into a fight. And of course, my parents blamed me for it. Tonight was about like the rest of today, which was one of the worst days of my life."

As he gently stroked the owl's feathers, tears brimmed in his eyes and splashed down his cheeks. He poured out his heart to the bird, describing in detail each wretched event, until he was sobbing again. The owl remained motionless, staring at him and blinking every once in a while.

Exhausted from the emotional outpouring, Keagen had begun to doze off when he heard an unfamiliar voice, deep, male, and calm.

"Thank you," the voice said.

Leaping to his feet, heart pounding, Keagen whirled around the room. "Who's there?" he choked out.

There was no answer. He settled back onto the bed, still very uneasy. "I'm not crazy," he thought. "I heard a voice, but I must have been dreaming." He sat there for another fifteen minutes, anxiety gradually giving way to drowsiness. He had just closed his eyes and put his head on the pillow when he heard it again.

"Master Keagen, I am sorry you are distraught." The voice was loud and clear. This time Keagen catapulted out of bed as if stung by a swarm of hornets. His eyes were wide open now, and he was shaking with fright. He grabbed a pencil from his nightstand and held it like a knife to defend himself. "Who—is—there?" he said, as bravely as he could.

"Slow down, my young friend," the voice replied calmly. "I am not here to hurt you. You saved my life today. I am in your debt."

Keagen's eyes widened. The sound seemed to be coming from the owl.

"Bubo, is that you? How? Ohhhh . . . " Keagen's thoughts were revving into overdrive. "This is how it starts, isn't it? I'm losing my mind. I'm going crazy!"

The owl blinked its orange eyes. "You are as sane as can be," the voice said, the bird's beak moving as it spoke.

"How are you doing this?" Keagen almost shouted. "How are you . . . talking to me?"

"There is more to us owls than meets the eye. If there is a valid reason, the barrier that prevents us from being able to speak to humans can be broken. I have never communicated with a human before. It's my first time, too."

Keagen's knees weakened, and he sank onto the bed, mouth agape.

"Thank you," the bird said again. "I collided with a very large vehicle, and I do not remember much after that, until you rescued me."

"Are you hurt?" Keagen asked. "Nothing seemed to be broken when I looked you over, but I'm no vet."

"I cannot move much. I know for certain that I cannot fly," Bubo said.

Keagen noticed the plate on the bed was empty and smiled. "But you can eat," he said. "How did you like the roast beef?"

"Less than satisfactory," the bird's voice said, "but I was so hungry, I did not have much choice." The orange eyes blinked.

"I'll try to figure out something more suitable for your diet."

"I would appreciate that," the owl replied.

"Why can I hear you?" Keagen went on. "It's crazy."

"That is not for me to say. I'm not really sure yet why the barrier was broken," Bubo replied. "You might inquire into why we met.

Why you found me, and why you chose to bring me to your home. I believe these things have happened for a reason."

"What reason?" The owl said nothing.

"This is nuts. I'm going to wake up tomorrow morning and find out this was all a dream," Keagen laughed as he tucked himself in beside Bubo. "I can't believe I'm talking to an owl! No, I can't believe I'm hearing an owl speak to me. Wait till I tell Waldo, Gina, and Didi!"

"May I give you some advice?" the owl's voice came again.

"Sure."

"Do not do that."

"Don't do what?" Keagen said.

"Tell your friends that you and I have had a conversation. They might indeed decide you are mad."

"Hmmm," Keagen said sleepily. "Good point."

CHAPTER FIVE

Mice on the Menu

Keagen opened his eyes and took a few seconds to orient himself. The clock radio beside his bed said 6:10 a.m. He sat up suddenly. The owl was still there and still not moving. Hesitantly, Keagen said, "Good morning to you, Bubo."

There was no answer.

"Ha! I knew it," he thought, with some disappointment. "Just a crazy dream. I really thought I could talk to an owl." He laughed out loud and started his morning routine, though in the back of his mind he wondered if it really *had* been a dream.

When he was ready for school, he said to the bird, "Don't go anywhere. Just relax and get better. And for the love of chocolate, please don't make any noise."

At school, Gina, Waldo, and DiDi could hardly believe Keagen was the same despondent boy from the day before. He daydreamed happily through Mr. Heldrich's math class, ignored the taunts of Franco and his gang, and managed to grit his way through the "extra training" that Coach Willard dished out for those students who had ranked as softies in the fitness assessment evaluations.

Toward the end of the day, Keagen pulled DiDi aside between classes and said, "I have something to show you. And I need your help."

An hour after school was out, DiDi was standing in Keagen's bedroom, beholding the feathered houseguest.

"He's enormous!" DiDi shouted. "And he's so tame. How did you get your mom to let you keep him in your room?"

"She doesn't know," Keagen confessed. "She only checks my room about once a week to be sure I'm keeping it clean, and she just did an inspection a few days ago. So I knew she probably wouldn't come in here. Isn't he beautiful? His name is Bubo."

Keagen had decided to keep his dream to himself for the time being, fearing DiDi would think the events of the previous day had driven his friend off the deep end.

DiDi wrinkled up his nose at the name, and then asked, "What are you feeding him?"

"That's where I need your help."

Keagen explained his plan for acquiring an appropriate owl diet. Bert had provided the materials for Keagen's concept of a mouse-trap—pieces of wood, bricks, sticks, and string, and Keagen had filched some cheese from the family icebox.

"We'll dig holes in the ground near the edge of the woods by the river and use the sticks to prop up a board and brick over each one," Keagen explained to DiDi. "Then we'll tie a string to the sticks and some cheese. When the mice grab the cheese—boom, the brick comes down and they are trapped!"

"I don't know, Keg—seems like real mousetraps would be an easier way to go, and more of a sure thing," DiDi argued.

"I don't have any money for mousetraps, and besides, I need the mice alive." The discussion was over, and after DiDi was sworn to secrecy, the friends headed for the fields to lay the traps. On his way out, Keagen whispered in a low voice to the owl, "Special for tomorrow night: *Mice a la Keagen*." Then he shivered in disgust.

The next day, both could not wait for school to be over to check for possible quarry. Keagen was astonished to discover that eight of the dozen holes he and DiDi had dug in the ground had imprisoned tiny field mice.

"Look at this!" Keagen blurted in disbelief. "It actually worked!"

"And now what?" DiDi asked.

"We take them home, of course. I'm sure Bubo is getting really tired of the leftover roast beef."

"But how? We don't have a box or anything to carry them in."

A little embarrassed by the oversight, Keagen looked around for something they could use to transport the mice. Suddenly he looked up with a smile that made DiDi uneasy. He knew that smile; it usually meant trouble.

"Give me your jacket," Keagen demanded.

"What? Are you crazy? My mom will kill me if something happens to this jacket."

"They're only going to be in there for a little while," Keagen pressed. "I'll use my jacket, too, but my pockets aren't big enough to fit all eight. How about if I take five and you take three? Come on, DiDi! Nothing will happen to your jacket, I promise."

"No way."

"Scared?" Keagen challenged him.

"You are nuts, you know that, Keagen? It's going to be your fault when my jacket ends up with little mouse holes chewed in it," he said, as he slowly pulled his arms out of the sleeves and handed the jacket over.

Keagen carefully removed each mouse by its tail and dropped it into a pocket of one jacket then the other, quickly closing the zippers to keep the wriggling, jumping creatures from escaping. At last all was secure, and they headed back to Keagen's house.

The next challenge was sneaking the squirming jackets past Keagen's mother and up to his room. They were in luck; she was in the basement doing laundry. "Perfect timing," Keagen thought with relief. The boys sprinted through the house and up the stairs. Dashing into Keagen's room, they slammed the door behind them with pounding hearts, pressing their backs against it as if being chased by disaster itself.

"Where?" DiDi shouted.

"What?" Keagen replied, out of breath.

"Where do you want to put them? I need to get them out of my jacket. They're wiggling like crazy!"

"Oh." Keagen scanned his room and was confronted with another gap in his plan. He hadn't thought about a cage or box in which to hold the mice.

Suddenly, footsteps. His mother must have heard them come in and was less than five seconds from entering his room to check on him. Without hesitating, Keagen tossed his jacket across the bed. It slipped from sight between the wall and the bed frame.

DiDi followed suit, but his aim was not as accurate as Keagen's. His jacket caught on the shade of the floor lamp in the corner, and as it dangled there, the pockets began to undulate as if they were hexed.

At that instant, his mother rapped on the door. "Keagen? Are you home? I thought I heard you come in." She pushed the door open. "Oh, hello, DiDi. I wasn't expecting company. Nice to see you again. How have you been?"

"Uh, fine," DiDi stammered, nervously adding, "I brought Keagen a report he needed for school. I was about to leave."

"Well, you're welcome to join us for dinner. Why don't you stay?"

"Thanks," he replied shyly. "But I should head back. I'm already late for dinner at my house. Maybe next time."

Keagen shifted his position to block his mother's view of the wildly moving jacket, still hanging from the lampshade. She pulled the door shut, and the boys were breathing a sigh of relief when it suddenly swung open again, and Keagen's mom stuck her head in once more.

"For goodness' sake, Keagen, open a window. Your room smells like wet dog," she said. "Haven't you been cleaning? I don't know how can you sleep in here," and she quickly disappeared again.

"Bubo!" Keagen thought with alarm. "I totally forgot about him." He looked around the room and finally spotted the owl sitting on the floor next to his bed, staring at them. Keagen noticed his feathers blended in almost completely with the carpet and dark wooden bedstead. Bubo had been in plain sight, yet his mother hadn't seen him.

He retrieved the two jackets and held them up triumphantly. "Breakfast, lunch, and dinner!" he announced. "No more cold roast beef for you, Bubo. What do you think?" The owl closed its eyes.

Keagen scoured the room again, searching for a suitable container for the mice. Then the satisfied smile returned, and he pulled the top drawer of his nightstand out completely, turned it over and dumped the contents unceremoniously on the floor. "Perfect," he said. He and DiDi then opened the zippered jacket pockets one by one and shook the mice out into the drawer, closing it quickly as soon as all eight inmates were safely relocated.

"Done!" Keagen said, with great satisfaction. "Bubo, as soon as I'm finished with dinner, it's your turn to snack, I promise. I won't be long." And both boys headed downstairs.

After DiDi departed, the family gathered at the dinner table. The meal was blessed, then everyone grabbed platters, bowls, and pots, filling their plates with minimal conversation and much clinking of cutlery.

After a few casual exchanges among the family members, Keagen's father was about to duck behind his newspaper again when Sallie let out a shrill scream that echoed through the house. She leaped up onto her chair, stuttering unintelligibly and pointing toward the staircase.

Keagen followed her terrified gaze and dropped his fork, staring in disbelief. Down the stairs came a line of little mice in perfect formation. As if by some prearranged plan, a pair headed into the living room, four went straight for the kitchen, and the final two came towards the dining room. Panic ensued.

"What in the world!" his father shouted over and over, while his mother joined Sallie in standing on her chair, gasping, shivering, and babbling, "We're infested! How could this happen? Todd, call the exterminators—call them now!"

"Darn!" Keagen thought as he helped his dad chase the mice, "brooming" them towards the front door. "I must have forgotten to shut the drawer all the way, or maybe I left the door to my room open." A bit irritated, he muttered under his breath, "Well, Bubo, no mice for you tonight."

CHAPTER SIX

Homecoming

"Wake up. Wake up! Wake up!" The distant voice became louder and louder, like a faraway train slowly approaching the platform.

Keagen felt a pinch on his nostrils and opened one eye. His vision was filled with a huge feathered head, punctuated by enormous orange eyes and a gigantic beak tugging his nose gently from side to side.

"Huh? What's happening? Bubo, what's the matter with you? Have you gone mental?" Keagen mumbled sleepily. He opened his other eye and stared blearily at the clock radio on the nightstand. It was 4:11 a.m. and pitch-dark outside. He sat up suddenly, switched on a light and looked down his nose at the owl, who was still attached and dangling from it.

Now panic swept over Keagen. "Are you okay? Are you hurt?" he almost shouted.

Bubo let go of the nose, found his balance and stretched his magnificent wings to their full span, extending well past the width of the bed. His glowing eyes, which were staring intently into Keagen's, radiated kindness and strength, and the boy felt not fear but an overwhelming sense of peace and trust as he gazed back.

"Ah, so you're talking to me again," Keagen said with a note of sarcasm, rubbing his nose with both hands. He had not heard the owl speak since the night he found the bird in the roadway. Over the two weeks since, Keagen had continued to sneak dinner leftovers up to Bubo and managed to keep his presence in the house a secret. Each evening he shared the events of his day with the owl, who seemed to listen closely, and Keagen could sense a strong bond developing between them. That Bubo suddenly chose to speak again seemed perfectly normal.

"What's the matter, my friend—can't sleep?" Keagen said softly. "Are you worried or thirsty?"

"Good morning, Master Keagen. Don't be concerned. I am well," the bird said. "Please get up and get dressed. We are going on an important journey today."

Keagen rubbed his eyes and made no attempt to stifle a big yawn. He looked down at the creature sitting beside him on the bed and realized suddenly that he had indeed begun to consider the owl a close friend.

"Bubo, first of all, please don't call me 'Mr. Keagen.' I'm only twelve and my name is just Keagen. People call my dad 'mister' and I never want to be called that, ever."

"I addressed you as Master Keagen, not 'Mister,'" the owl corrected. "'Master' is a commonly accepted, traditional title for school-age males. It is perfectly appropriate for our interactions."

Keagen gave him a puzzled look, then shrugged his shoulders and pointed to the clock radio.

"And for the love of chocolate, do you see those red numbers? They mean I still have lots of time to sleep because it's Saturday, and I don't have to go to that stupid school today."

"School is anything but stupid, Master Keagen . . . you will see. But as I said, we have a fair distance to cover today. We must get started now."

Keagen hesitated. "Where do you want me to go in the middle of the night, and what will my mother say when I don't come down for breakfast, and she finds I'm not in my bed?"

"You will write a note to your mother saying that you have gone to the forest near your school to work on a nature project, and that you will be back in the afternoon."

"A *nature* project?" Keagen looked at the owl skeptically.

"You must trust me, Master Keagen," Bubo replied. "That is exactly what you will be participating in. Get dressed, write the message to your mother, and quietly collect some of the food you like to eat—sandwiches, fruit, and the cookies your mother bakes. I rather like those, so include more than a few. Pack a bag and get your bicycle. It is time for you to meet my family and the world I call home."

"Really?" Keagen almost shouted in excitement and jumped out of bed, bumping into Bubo and sending him careening sideways onto the floor, flapping his wings furiously to regain his balance. Bubo puffed his feathers and shook his head in obvious disgust and disapproval, but Keagen paid no attention. He began pulling on his jeans, almost losing his balance in the process. "Did I hear this right? I'm going to meet your family? I didn't know you *had* a family! I get to take you home?"

The words had barely come out of his mouth when Keagen froze, all the joy and excitement gone in an instant, as it dawned on him what this meant. Cold fear gripped his spine, and he felt as if he'd been hit full-force in the stomach. Bubo was healed and back to normal. He wanted to go home for good, and that meant leaving Keagen behind. The closest friend he'd ever had, gone like some amazing dream.

Keagen fell backwards onto the end of his bed. He thought he would faint. Recognizing his distress, Bubo flapped up from the floor to Keagen's lap, just inches from his face.

"But . . . I thought you *were* home," the boy choked out. "This is your home, I'm your home. You are the only one who's ever really listened and understood me. You are my dearest friend, and I love you so much. You can't just go away. I saved you. You belong to me."

The owl's voice was firm, but soothing. "Master Keagen, it is true you saved me. You cared for me, and I share your affection and the bond between us. But even so, I do not belong to you, nor do you belong to me. Great friendship doesn't belong to anyone; it just is, no matter where we are. I have a life that makes me happy. I miss my home and family and am eager to return to them. But do you think once you take me back we will never see each other again? That we would wave a casual good-bye and part ways as if our friendship never existed?

"I do not know why the barrier of language between our species was broken, but I am grateful for it. You are an amazing young man with fine qualities far beyond your own comprehension. You have a pure, beautiful soul and the strength to make a meaningful difference in the lives of others, maybe even in this world. I know you can't see that yet, but you must trust me. There is a reason we met."

Keagen sat motionless. He had never heard anyone speak about him in such a way. Huge tears filled his eyes and splashed down his face.

Bubo gently shifted position to brush his head against Keagen's cheek. Then he unfolded his gigantic wings and wrapped them around the boy, until the tips touched and Keagen was entirely engulfed in owl feathers. Time stood still as the friends embraced.

"No, Master Keagen," Bubo's voice finally said softly. "This is not the end. This is just the beginning."

Keagen nodded slightly. At last, he accepted it. Bubo wanted to go home. What choice did he have but to support the wishes of his friend?

The March wind blew cold as the two of them headed out of the house and toward the forest. Keagen was glad he had grabbed his jacket at the last minute. He couldn't see Bubo as he pedaled along but heard the contact between wings and wind right above his head. It was getting close to 5:30 a.m., and he could barely make out the road in the dim, predawn light. He hoped the note to his mother would do the trick, so that she didn't send the police in search of him. If it didn't work, his father would put him in a home for orphans—at least, that's what he always said anytime Keagen got into trouble. Keagen knew he meant it as part-frustrated joke, part-empty threat, but it always made him feel uncomfortable. At the moment, though, none of that mattered. He was with his best friend in the world, and they were off on an adventure.

With Bubo leading, they turned from the road into the woods, following a path that went from good to bad to nonexistent. Soon Keagen had to get off his bike and push it over rocks and tree roots, across rutted sections of the disappearing trail. The deep emerald forest canopy was spread out above him, beautiful and a bit spooky all at the same time. As the first sunlight broke through the tree branches, it filtered down like hundreds of spotlights ready to show-case the woodland performers.

Birds began to chirp, and soon other animals added their unique voices to the choir, with the wind providing a restful undertone to the harmonic celebration of a new day. Fallen leaves and pine needles created a soft carpet beneath Keagen's feet, and with each step he could smell the calming aroma of rich, moist earth, fresh rain, pinesap, and wild mushrooms. The tree stumps and broken branches that were scattered on either side and sometimes across the faded path seemed to have been placed there with great intention and design to complete the exquisite landscape.

Roughly twenty minutes after they entered the forest, it gave way to a large, almost rectangular open field, surrounded on all sides by trees. A small stream cut through the rich green grass of the clearing, entering from the top as if drawing a breath of fresh air and then exhaling at the lower end as it disappeared back into the hidden reaches of the woods.

In the middle of the field was a single, majestic tree, standing strong and powerful, like the ruler of a kingdom who had been dropped onto a throne from above. Its dark branches reached up as if to touch the orange cotton candy clouds reflecting the sun's early morning glow. Keagen surveyed the scene in awe. "So this is Bubo's home," he thought. "Beautiful, *absolutely beautiful!*"

Noticing Keagen's delight, the owl said, "Lovely, isn't it? We call it 'Owls' Meadow.' I'm glad you like it, Keagen."

As they approached the tree, animals of all types and sizes came out from every corner of the forest, rushing towards them and surrounding Bubo in a joyous welcome. Keagen stared in wonder at the menagerie: a beaver family, fourteen raccoons, several porcupines, a pair of grass snakes, an otter family, a fox, a group of squirrels, countless birds, and a rabbit with nine baby bunnies. Then there were the owls—at least a dozen, all clustered protectively around Bubo.

The chattering, chirping, hooting, screeching, and barking was almost deafening. Keagen was taken aback by the way Bubo was celebrated. "He must be a great friend to many in his world," he thought. "I wouldn't have any idea how it feels to have that many friends. He is truly amazing."

Keagen sat down so as not to tower over the gathering. As he did so, the owl closest to Bubo, which looked like a smaller version of his friend, moved in his direction. He felt a bit uneasy, as he didn't know this owl, and froze when the huge bird climbed into his lap. Its head was very close to his, and the large beak almost touched his nose. The huge orange eyes stared right into him without a blink. Keagen didn't move or dare to breathe.

Suddenly the owl touched its head to Keagen's cheek, and for the second time that day, massive wings wrapped around him, covering his upper body with a feather blanket that felt safe and secure.

In a soft, feminine voice the owl said, "How can I ever thank you for rescuing Baron and returning him home to us? He is the center of our world, and by saving him, in many ways, you saved us, too."

Keagen gasped and drew back in surprise. Another owl was speaking to him? And *Baron*? Did she call him Baron?

The owl released him, and he heard her chuckle. "I'm sorry, I should have introduced myself," she said. "My name is Salomona, and Baron von Hoppe is my mate. We were all so worried when he did not come home—I feared for his life. We had almost given up hope. Thank you, thank you, thank you!"

Keagen's face reddened. "He's . . . a baron?" he said slowly, swallowing hard. "I was calling him Bubo."

Salomona blinked and shook her head. "I'm not surprised he didn't tell you. He doesn't set much store by titles. For being the leader he is in the forest community, sometimes Baron's modesty amazes me."

More owls flew in from all directions, and it became clear to Keagen that he was able to hear and communicate with every owl, but with the owls alone.

After a few minutes, the conversation ceased and everyone looked up into the sky to the north. Keagen could see a tiny speck becoming larger and larger as another bird approached rapidly. Its graceful, powerful moves reminded him of an eagle or a falcon. When it came closer, though, he identified the body shape unquestionably as that of another owl, though this one was much smaller than any of the others and pearl white, reflecting the sunlight like the tip of a mountain covered in snow.

The owl touched down and embraced Baron with overwhelming joy and happiness. Baron turned to Keagen, and with deep love in his eyes and pride in his voice said, "Keagen, meet our daughter, Emmanuella. We call her LaLa."

The owl had exquisite, yellow-orange eyes shaped like almonds and feather whiskers that stood straight up above the eyebrows like a royal crown. Keagen was amazed by her beauty and also a bit confused about how different she looked from Baron and Salomona.

Noticing his perplexed frown, LaLa started to laugh. "Keagen, it is wonderful to meet you," she said in a charming voice. "And thank you so much for all you have done for my father. The entire forest is speaking about you and your bravery. You are a hero in our world."

"A hero?" Keagen mouthed the words blankly. No one had ever called him that before—ever. He blushed at the unfamiliar sense of pride the words caused.

Baron came up to him and said, "LaLa is a very special snowy owl. We brought her home from a faraway land to become part of our family. She is our greatest pride and a princess in her own right."

Keagen started to ask a question, but Baron stopped him. "Later, my friend. We have much time to share our stories. For now, I would like to introduce you to the rest of our little group."

As Keagen looked around the circle of animals in the clearing, he realized he had never felt safer or more like he belonged than in that very moment.

CHAPTER SEVEN

Back in the Conference Room

Saturday, 9:28 a.m.

Dalton paused in his narrative to drink a glass of water. The room was absolutely silent. Looking around the conference table, he saw nothing but disbelief in every person's eyes, save one. SVP Joseph Walt sat back comfortably in his chair, arms crossed over his chest, a self-satisfied smile on his face. His relaxed demeanor did not go unnoticed by Susan Richards, the vice president of accounting, who was seated directly across from Walt. She had the impression Walt and this man knew each other. "Is this a set-up?" she thought. "Something's going on here. I can feel it."

Tom Murray, vice president of global sales, was the first to break the silence. "Mr. Dickson," he began.

"Dalton, that is," Dalton corrected him.

"Ahem, yes, sorry," Murray went on. "Mr. Dalton. You seem like a nice old man, but we don't know who you are or how you came to find us. You are obviously at the wrong location and may be a bit confused. We are waiting for a consultant to arrive, and that person is clearly not you. I just received a text from Mr. Ulrich that the consultant's name is Goodwin, Jack Goodwin. So, you are interrupting a very important meeting, and frankly, we have no time to listen to your ridiculous, albeit charming, children's story. Please sir, leave now before I have to call security."

Dalton was unfazed by the threat and smiled broadly. "*Am* I in the wrong place, Mr. Murray?" he asked. "Are you sure it is I who's lost? And how can you be so certain what I've told you so far is a children's story? By the way," he added, "Mr. Goodwin will not be joining us today. I'm afraid you'll have to settle for me. You see, Mr. Murray—and I'm speaking not only to you when I say this—I'm rather disappointed, though not surprised, by what you've said.

"You sounded quite bossy and in charge just now, yet you weren't so secure and confident when Mr. Ulrich was here earlier today. If I understand correctly, the only person who stood up to Ulrich was Joe Walt, even though he knew doing so might come with negative consequences. You're talking a big game now with someone you think you can intimidate, but when push came to shove in the heat of the earlier confrontation, you chose to take the fifth and keep your mouth shut. If you want to impress *me*, Mr. Murray, you'll have to do better than that. I'm not judging you, or placing blame. But one of the things a consultant does is point out the obvious. You cannot un-ring that bell. No matter how you look at it, none of you, with the exception of Mr. Walt, made a stand."

Karl Ruttner, the senior vice president of marketing, leaped to his feet and marched up to Dalton. "You've got a lot of nerve talking to us that way!" he almost shouted. "How do you know what happened in our meeting with Ulrich? You weren't here. Besides, you know nothing about our situation. And who do you think you are to make up some crazy story about the founder of Hoppe Enterprises talking to owls? That's who your story is about, right? Keagen Walkabee?" His face, by now quite red, was inches away from Dalton's.

"You've noticed, I'm sure," Dalton said calmly, "that the Hoppe Enterprises logo incorporates the figure of an owl. Did you ever wonder why?"

This further infuriated Ruttner, but before he could splutter a reply, Joseph Walt cut in. "Let's hear the rest of what he has to say, Karl," Walt said firmly. "I think we should see where this is going. We certainly have nothing to lose but a little more time. Then we can throw him out." Walt's eyes twinkled.

Ruttner started to object, then turned and stormed back to his seat. Walt glanced around at the group, but there were no further comments. "Please continue, Mr. Dalton," Walt said, and Dalton resumed his story.

Lessons at the Little Stream

Weeks went by, and Keagen became a frequent visitor to Owls' Meadow. He loved spending the warm spring days after school and on weekends with the animals. Listening with interest to the stories the owls told, he learned much of their traditions and heritage, and about day-to-day life in the forest.

Best of all was the time he spent in Baron's company. Keagen had the distinct feeling Baron was in his head, understanding perfectly what was happening in his life.

One particularly balmy afternoon, Keagen stretched out on a river rock protruding from the bank of the small brook that flowed through the glade. The stream's icy water cooled the gentle breeze that blew across it, giving the air a crisp, refreshing edge.

He watched as Baron lighted comfortably on a nearby gnarled tree root, adjusted his wings and began preening with his beak. He first shook his entire body to ruffle all the feathers, then quickly and efficiently settled each one back into its rightful place. The effect was as if he had been brushed until he gleamed. The owl's pride in his elegant, well-groomed appearance was one of the many things Keagen had come to admire about him.

Baron always seemed so confident and in control, Keagen thought. He marveled once again that a creature of such magnificence was truly his best friend, whom he loved dearly.

The two sat in silence for a bit, with Keagen pretending to doze on the sunny stone. Then Baron said softly, "Keagen." The boy had finally convinced his mentor to drop the formal "Master" when addressing him.

"Hmmm?" Keagen mumbled.

"May I ask you a personal question?"

"Of course." Keagen opened his eyes and looked curiously at Baron. "What's up?"

"Why are you so keen to become someone you were not meant to be?"

"What are you talking about?"

"Those boys at your school—the ones who excel at sports and are so 'rough-and-tumble.' I sense that your heart is heavy, and you berate yourself because you are not like them. It's as if you believe you are not good enough."

"You are right," Keagen said. "They are better than me."

Baron fluffed up his feathers and said sharply, "Do not twist my words. That is not at all what I said."

"But they *are*," Keagen persisted. "It's okay if you say it. Even my father thinks I'm a loser."

"Has he ever told you that?"

"Not in those exact words, but I can feel it. I can tell by how he acts that's what he's thinking. Otherwise, why would he speak more highly about the neighbor boys and their perfect standing than about me? Once I heard him say to my mom, "Our boy is different, and I don't know what we did wrong.""

"You are making assumptions," Baron said.

"Well, I'm *right*!" Keagen shouted, leaping off the rock to crouch beside the stream. "But one day I'll prove to him he was wrong all along, and that I'm somebody special. I'll show him who I really am. He'll be sorry, but maybe I won't accept his apology. Maybe it'll just be too late."

"Ah," Baron said. "So you think you are only of value to others if you have proven yourself in some way and shown them you are worthy. Maybe by doing something 'cool,' as you call it, something that garners much praise, or that makes a lot of money, perhaps?"

"Yep, that should shut them up."

"And once you have proven yourself, other people will respect you?"

"They'd better." Keagen picked up a handful of pebbles and flung them into the water.

"I see," Baron said. "You command respect through acts of entitlement, and once others respect you, then you can start to respect yourself. Don't you think you might have the formula backwards here, Keagen? You concern yourself far too much with what others think, and you compare yourself to boys some of whose ways of behavior offer you nothing I can see worth taking on as a practice in your life. That reminds me—have you ever heard the tale of 'The Spider and the Crabs?'"

"Not that I remember." Keagen was by now accustomed to Baron's fondness for using stories to teach him lessons, but he was in no mood for one after this conversation.

"It's a parable you could consider and possibly learn from," Baron continued. "A spider became acquainted with a group of river crabs, and he was jealous because he wanted to be like them. He admired the crabs for their speed and the strength of their claws, and most of all, because they were able to walk under water. He thought there was something wrong with him because he didn't have these capabilities, and he felt like an outsider.

"The crabs knew the spider was actually much stronger than they were, much faster and had far more talents—such as the ability to spin an amazing web—yet they still made fun of him. Because he didn't realize his own power and abilities, it was easy for them to intimidate and control him. The spider began to believe that because he couldn't do the things they could do, he wasn't worth much.

"As the days went by, the spider watched them closely, imitating their behavior and the way they moved in hopes of one day being accepted. Eventually he started to believe he *was* like them, and the crabs dared him to prove it by jumping into the river and walking under water. Desperate to show them he was worthy, he took their dare, and as you can imagine, that was the end of the spider."

"I don't like that story," Keagen said. "And besides, I think you made it up just to prove you're right."

"Do you understand the message behind it?" Baron asked gently. "You cannot become someone you are not. In fact, you are not supposed to be like everyone else. You are unique, with your own qualities and talents. Others won't respect you for trying to bend yourself to fit in. If you are not willing to discover who you really are, you will always be looking for the approval of others. Today it's your dad or the students and teachers at school, tomorrow it will be someone you work for. And you will never stop trying to convince them you are worthy.

"Eventually you will discover that you are living and acting solely to please others, forgetting completely who you are and what you stand for. Your entire life will be spent chasing after something you will never find."

Keagen, who was now using a stick to dig into the dirt of the riverbank, didn't respond.

Baron went on. "Everything that you are starts and ends with you. Respect is gained when you choose to be, think, and act true to your own self. When you stand for your personal values, others might not like you for it, and they might not agree with you, but they will respect you for taking that stand. Don't try to impress others by striving to be who you think you should be in their eyes. Rather, impress them with who you really are. Become more like the ocean. The ocean doesn't care what people say. The ocean just is."

A slight smile crossed Keagen's lips, and he nodded.

"You will find cruel, dishonorable, and dangerous people everywhere you go," Baron continued. "They are out there, in the world. So running away, or hoping things will get better once you are done with school is simply wishful thinking. There is, however, something you can do right now that will make a difference in your life. Choose not to be impacted by others who unleash their own insecurities on you. You see, Keagen, the mean kids who mistreat you are getting their self-confidence at your expense. It makes them feel important to push others down.

"They try to cover up their feelings of inadequacy by making others fear them, when in reality they are the ones who are lost. I advise you to ignore them, laugh at them, feel sorry for them, and stop feeding them your fear. If you want to emulate others, look for people who are worthy of being imitated. Find the good ones; they are out there, too. Know who your true friends are. You already have several in your life—DiDi, Gina, and Waldo, for example. From what you have told me, I like them very much. You can be yourself with them. They stand behind you and watch your back, as you do theirs.

"I love that old saying, 'Show me your friends, and I will show you your future.' Your true friends will give you the confidence to know you are indeed special and important. You just have to listen more carefully to them and recognize they already respect you a great deal. Why do you ignore the opinions of the ones who care about you and pay more attention to those who make you feel bad about yourself and ill-treat you? Too often it is the real friend who gets overlooked because we don't have any idea just how much that person looks out for us. Everyone has that friend."

Baron then swooped gracefully from the tree root to the river rock, to be closer to Keagen. "I understand that it is important to feel accepted and equal. And I know you have been tormented by some very tough lads. It's no fun to be ridiculed and treated like an outsider, but as long as you believe in yourself, you are wearing an armor that will protect you from most of their attacks."

"What do you know about being treated like an outsider?" Keagen replied hoarsely, without looking up. "You are a baron, high in the ranks of your world. I've seen how others respect you. They look up to you, and everyone likes you."

"Do they?" Baron replied, with a trace of humor in his voice. "Well, well, then you know something I don't. I have enemies, too, Keagen. There are those who are jealous of my leadership, some of them even dangerous, who, given the opportunity, would not hesitate to hurt me and my family. But we have learned who we can trust and who we cannot, and I suggest you start doing the same. Don't ever trust someone just because they tell you to. That's a mistake that can have fatal consequences. Learn to listen to your instincts. You have them, you know."

Keagen finally met Baron's gaze but could think of nothing to say.

"Have you ever heard the story of the 'Turtle and the Scorpion?'"

"*Another* animal story?" Keagen said, not attempting to hide his sarcasm.

Baron ignored the remark and said, "This one comes from the oral tradition of our Tongan fore-owls and was told to me by my paternal grand-owl himself. It's an old fable whose lesson has served me well through my years.

"Long ago, in the forest of a distant land, a turtle approached a river and prepared to cross a deep passage. Suddenly a scorpion came out of the bushes of the riverbank and shouted to the turtle. 'Wait up . . . please wait! Would you give me a lift over the river to the other side?'

"The turtle hesitated. 'Why would I do that? You are a scorpion; your sting is highly poisonous. You could easily end my life.'

"The scorpion replied in a calm, soothing voice. 'I have asked you for help. I don't sting those who help me.'

"But the turtle was not convinced. 'You are a powerful, dangerous creature, and I am just a helpless turtle. I've been told your kind cannot be trusted. It's said you speak words others want to hear when you are out to get something, then you sting as soon as you don't need them anymore.'

"'No, no,' the scorpion replied. 'You are mistaken, dear turtle. Idle, uninformed talk has given me an undeserved reputation. Why would I try to harm you? You are a strong, brave swimmer, and I have only asked kindly for your help to cross the river. I need you; I have no reason to harm you. You can trust me.'

"The turtle thought about the scorpion's flattering words and was persuaded by his cajoling manner. Finally, against her better judgement, she gave in.

"'All right,' the turtle said. 'Climb on and hold tight.' The scorpion crawled onto the turtle's back, and she slid gently into the river. The passage was smooth, and the scorpion cheered the turtle for her great skill and immense kindness. Once they were safely on the other side, the scorpion skittered to the ground and turned. With a lightning-fast move, he sank his stinger into the turtle's neck just above her shell and released his poison.

"The turtle was stunned. She couldn't believe what had just happened. 'Why did you do that?' she mumbled in shock and disbelief. 'You stung me. Your poison will kill me. You promised you wouldn't harm me.'

"'Yes, I did, but I'm still a scorpion,' said he, casually. 'It's in my nature.' And he sauntered off, leaving the turtle to her fate."

Keagen was quiet for some time after Baron had finished, glowering angrily as he processed the moral of the tale. Finally, he said,

"That's a terrible story. It's sad and wrong. How could the scorpion be so mean? Show me that scorpion; I'll smash it with my shoe."

Baron watched calmly as Keagen cooled off. "It's a fable, Keagen, not a real event. It illustrates a point that can be translated into many situations."

"Well," Keagen snapped back, "whatever a fable is, I don't like it. What the scorpion did stinks and makes me mad."

Baron suppressed a chuckle. "That's one of the things I love most about you, Keagen," he said. "You have a very pure sense of right and wrong, of which I hope you shall never lose sight. Now just apply that clear sense of judgement to the people in your world and decide who is the turtle and who is the scorpion."

The owl paused for a moment, deep in thought, then said, "I think that is what most separates the animal and human worlds. Humans are constantly trying to change each other, and if they can't ac- complish that, they then try to control others, often with fear or force.

"Imagine the chaos if the animals in the kingdom told each other who they should be and how they should behave, to the point where they actually began to believe it. Each species knows where we stand with every other. We anticipate, calculate, and respect each other's values, motives, and actions. We do not try to turn a rabbit into an eagle or a crocodile into a dolphin. We accept them for who they are, because we truly have no other option. We enjoy our friends with love and support, and we know from whom we had better stay away. The outcomes of our interactions are always consequences of the quality of our choices."

"You know, Baron," Keagen said thoughtfully, "I'm just twelve. I'm not a college professor or a high scholar. I think I follow you, but it would help if you could explain your point so even I could get it."

"Hmmm . . . yes, I see. Wait here. I'll be back. I want to show you something." With that, Baron spread his powerful wings and disappeared into the nearby trees. Minutes later he appeared again, his huge body sailing weightless on the wind, and touched down lightly in the exact spot from which he had taken off. He tucked back his massive wings, then fluffed and smoothed his feathers.

Keagen noticed he had a piece of crumpled paper in his beak. Baron dropped it on the ground, and Keagen's eyes widened. "Wow!" he said. "Is that what I think it is?"

"This is a fifty-dollar bill, I believe," Baron said.

Keagen stared in disbelief. "That's a lot of money."

"Would you like to have it?"

"Are you kidding?" The boy was almost beside himself. "My weekly allowance is fifteen cents. I've never seen so much money. Where did you get it?"

"We owls have good eyes. We find things all the time."

Keagen was puzzled. How could someone lose fifty dollars?

"You *found* it?" he said.

"Yes. Would you like to have it?" Baron asked again.

Keagen was in awe. "I . . . no, it's too much. I can't accept it."

"Nonsense," Baron countered. "I would have used it to help build a nest for LaLa's babies, when the time comes, but I can find other material with which to do that. To us it has no more value than that of the paper. Please take it. And besides, look at its condition. It's a bit damaged; it's torn, has gotten wet, and looks as if it has been stomped upon. It surely doesn't have the value of fifty dollars anymore."

"Of course it does!" Keagen almost shouted.

"Why is that?" Baron asked. "It is worn and abused. I'm sure people did not treat it with sensitivity, respect, or kindness. There is no way it still has the full value."

"But it *does*!" Keagen insisted, his voice rising almost an octave.

"Ah," Baron said. "That's odd. You are telling me that money holds its value even when it's being bullied?"

Keagen looked confused.

"Didn't you just say that you are of lesser value because of how you have been treated and what others think of you? They make you believe you are not good enough, and as a result, your value changes from fifty dollars to fifty cents? Please explain that to me."

"It's not the same thing," Keagen began.

"Isn't it?" Baron countered. "It's all in your mind, Keagen. You only lose your personal value if you allow it. If this fifty dollar bill could feel, it probably would be hurt by the way it was treated and believe its value had diminished to that of a lesser note. But because it can't feel, its value is not affected by the way others handle it. Imagine how different things would be if you chose not to be hurt by others' comments and opinions. You would likely maintain your sense of value, too."

This was a bit over Keagen's head, and he sat quietly contemplating the meaning of it all. He mostly loved the way Baron explained things, using examples and never belittling or making Keagen feel stupid if he didn't understand at first. But sometimes Baron went pretty far out to make a point.

At that moment, a white flash shot from the sky and almost collided with Keagen, missing his left shoulder by less than an inch. He couldn't see what the object was but felt the draft of wind as it sped past him.

"What in the world?" Keagen shouted, stunned. "What *was* that?"

Baron sat still as a marble statue, wide-eyed. "That was LaLa," he murmured.

"LaLa?" Keagen looked up into the sky but saw nothing. "Why did she attack me?"

"I don't think that was the case, Keagen. I'm not sure what just happened. Perhaps she was practicing her flying skills. I will investigate and let you know."

Keagen stood up and dusted off the back of his pants. "Well, maybe this was a sign. It's time for me to be getting back anyway."

"Take the fifty-dollar bill, but with it, I ask one favor."

"Of course," Keagen said. "What's that?"

"Don't spend it."

"What? Why?"

Baron fluttered up to a tree branch so that he was at eye level with Keagen. "If you choose to spend it, the money will be gone within a few weeks, and you'll have nothing left. I'm requesting you keep it to remind you of our conversation about the true worth of an individual. Anytime someone tries to lower your self-esteem, look at the bill and remember my words."

"But that's a lot of money. I could really use it."

"If you take my message to heart, you will earn many more of those bills, most likely far more than you can count. But for now, I'm asking you to hold onto this one. Do you accept my request?"

"I guess so," Keagen said reluctantly, shoving the bill into his pocket. "See ya tomorrow, Baron. And tell LaLa to cool her jets." He jumped on his bike and headed into the woods.

At dusk that evening, Baron and Salomona were sitting side by side on a large branch outside their tree trunk home when LaLa descended from the sky, landing near them.

"Well," Baron said. "Any more flying stunts today?"

"I know, *I know*," LaLa said, her sweet voice filled with apology. "That was much closer than I thought it would be."

"You almost flattened Keagen and frightened him besides," Baron said. "Impact at that speed would have seriously injured both of you."

"I'm sorry, Dad, but I had no choice," LaLa replied. "It was right behind him and about to strike when I saw it. If I hadn't made the dive, I would have been too late."

"A snake?"

"A viper," she said.

"The most dangerous of all." Baron paused, furrowing the feathers over his brow. "Keagen would probably not have survived the bite."

"No," LaLa said softly. "I was heading out when I saw you two near the stream. Then I noticed the grass moving behind Keagen's back. I wasn't sure at first, then it lifted its head to get ready to strike. I had no time to think and dropped into a free fall."

"LaLa, you saved his life," Baron said quietly.

"Just as he saved yours."

"Such a risk," Salomona chimed in worriedly. "Vipers are deadly for us, too. They're lighting-fast and hate owls. You are very lucky."

"I came out of the sun. Once the snake saw me, it was too late. Besides, it was so focused on Keagen that I had the advantage. Does Keagen know why I almost hit him?"

"No," Baron said. "I told him you were practicing your flying skills."

LaLa laughed. "Okay. Let's keep this incident to ourselves. No need to scare him unnecessarily. When I see him, I'll apologize and acknowledge my flying ability obviously needs work."

The three moved closer together on the tree branch and contentedly watched the arrival of nightfall.

CHAPTER NINE

You Don't Lose Until You Show Defeat

"So!" Baron's urgent tone caught Keagen off-guard. He had just arrived at the big tree in the clearing and was dismounting from his bicycle.

"So . . . what?" he asked hesitantly.

"Big day tomorrow, yes?" Baron said.

"Huh? What big day?"

"The baseball tryouts. You will be participating, correct?"

"Baron, that's not even a little bit funny. Quit trying to be humorous. It doesn't suit you."

"My comment was not intended as a joke, Keagen," Baron said slowly and deliberately. "I meant it, and in fact, I ask that you take part in the tryouts. I want you to go."

"Why? You know what will happen. They'll laugh at me as soon as I walk onto the field, and that will be just the beginning." Keagen crumpled down into a heap among the tree's enormous roots. "Here's the crazy thing—I don't even blame them. I *do* suck at baseball, and that's the truth."

"But you like baseball, don't you?"

"That has nothing to do with the fact that I have a lousy throw, can't run fast even if my life depends on it, and I'm even worse at catching. They will be in my face!"

"Stop being such an easy target. You accept your limitations rather easily, Keagen. There may be boys with more talent than you, but in the end, it is passion for the game that prevails. Skill alone doesn't make a great athlete. It also takes heart. Skills can be developed."

"Look at me, Baron. Do I look like an athlete? Even if I had worked hard on getting better—even if my dad had helped me—there was never any chance for me to make the team."

"Ah, I see." Baron fluffed up then smoothed down his feathers, preparing for a challenge. "So you think trying something new only makes sense if winning and acceptance are guaranteed? Listen to yourself, Keagen. This is not about baseball. This is about giving up before you even get started. You will never learn how it feels to really win until you begin to challenge your inner fear. How many times a day do you say to yourself, 'Why should I attempt that, if I know I'm not good at it anyway, and I know I'm going to fail?' That is destructive thinking, Keagen, and it is time for you to change the direction of your thoughts."

"Easy for you to say," Keagen shot back, "Impossible for me to do."

Baron was losing patience. "I insist that you avoid using those permanent words," he said. "There is no such thing as 'always', 'never', 'impossible', or 'endless'. They are created concepts that don't actually exist."

"Okay then, how do I change the way I am?"

"You misunderstand, Keagen. You cannot change the way you are, but you can certainly shift the core of how you think about things. Change the question. Ask yourself, 'Why not give it a try, for all it's worth?' For heaven's sake, that's why it's called a tryout!"

Keagen sighed. "You always make things sound so simple, Baron. You are the greatest friend I could have ever imagined, but you are a . . . baron. You are good at everything. Doesn't seem to me you've ever failed much."

"I have failed at many things I have attempted," Baron replied, "and I have attempted many things. I've had hard times to overcome and experienced numerous disappointments and setbacks. But these only count as 'failures' if I accept them as such. Each time I failed, I stood back up, looked to see what I could learn, and then let go of my fear that I might fail again. The only difference between us, Keagen, is that I refused to give up. Letting go of our fear is not at all the same thing as giving up. Thinking we cannot do something becomes a self-fulfilling prophecy. It creates a condition that predetermines the outcome: defeat."

"So, losing and being embarrassed are *good* things?" Keagen couldn't help the sarcasm, even though he risked being disrespectful.

"Keagen, I notice that you walk very well."

"What? Where did that question come from?"

"Could you walk the moment you were born?"

"Baron—really?" Keagen hesitated, but Baron was waiting for an answer. "Of course not. Nobody can."

"So you could not walk as an infant, but all of a sudden one day, you discovered there was more to movement than just crawling on all fours. You tried to stand, pulling up on everything you could get your hands on, and then you tried to walk. How many times do you think you fell on your behind before you were successful? Thousands, perhaps? But you did not give up because you knew it was possible, and your instincts were guiding you.

"You didn't care whether the baby next door had started to walk, and it didn't matter to you that your parents laughed when you hit the ground again and again. Soon you were walking, and then running, with great skill and efficiency. If you'd had the same attitude then as you have today, you would be still crawling."

"Where are you going with this, Baron?" Keagen was tiring of the conversation.

"Have you ever heard of the '96 Percent/4 Percent Rule?'" Baron asked.

"Sounds like a math thing, and you know I'm not good at math."

Baron continued undeterred. "Ninety-six percent of individuals hope they will be considered important once they become successful. The other four percent understand they are *already* important, and that winning and being successful are just by-products of who they already are."

"You are serious, aren't you? You really do want me to go to the tryouts tomorrow."

"I could not be more sincere in my request."

"You know how this will end, don't you?"

Baron settled on the boy's extended forearm and looked into his eyes. "You may or may not make the team. You may or may not get picked on. Regardless, I want you to promise me three things."

"What three things?"

"First, don't attend the tryouts feeling pressured that you *must* make the team. Remember that baseball is a game, and a game should be fun. Don't beat yourself up if you miss a ball. Recover with ease, and go at it again. You are not there to prove anything. Enjoy yourself!

"Two, give your very best. Even if you are not selected, you will know at the end of the day you put absolutely everything you had into your effort.

"Three, should you not make the team, don't leave the field with slouching shoulders and a drooping chin. Depart with pride and contentedness. Don't feel defeated, and you won't show defeat. Walk up to the players who made the team, shake their hands, and congratulate them. Wear a smile, speak with genuine passion, and look each person straight in the eye. Wish them a successful season, and tell them you will root for them."

"No way!" Keagen shouted. "Bad enough you ask me to throw myself to the wolves just by trying out. I'm not about to feed their egos, too. Why are you doing this?"

"The question you should be asking is, 'Why not?'" Baron said. "You claim you are not respected by others. Well, let me explain how you can change that, and it has little to do with whether or not you make the team. Respect is given to people who try new things beyond their comfort zone, show courage, and give it their best, regardless of winning or losing. The most successful individuals have not become champions because they won every time. All of them had to learn to deal with great obstacles and setbacks. They had to learn to face their fears head-on. That is how winning is done.

"We all have the opportunity to choose between two paths, Keagen. One is the way taken by those who are willing to seek out and confront the things they are most afraid of. The other way is of those who respond to a challenge by hiding or running away.

"The path you follow becomes part of who you are and will impact just about everything—the friends you make, the life partner you choose and family you create, the work you take on, your hobbies and interests—every aspect of your life."

"You're pretty sure I'm not going to make the team, aren't you?"

"Of course I hope you will make the team. But that is entirely beside the point," Baron said. "Have you heard anything I've said?"

Keagen finally gave in. "Okay. If it's so important to you that I do this, even if it destroys me—so be it. Speak kindly at my funeral."

"You are being overly dramatic, don't you think?" Baron said.

"No actually, that was an understatement. I hope they have paramedics in the dugout."

Keagen did not sleep much that night, worrying, tossing, and turning hour after hour. He envisioned countless scenarios for how the next day might go, but they all led to the same inevitable outcome: humiliation, defeat, peals of derisive laughter, and the complete destruction of life as he knew it.

Finally the buzzer on his alarm clock went off, jolting him into the reality that the day of reckoning had actually arrived. He slowly rolled out of bed and walked to the closet to gather his baseball practice clothes. As he stuffed them and his mitt into his backpack, he caught a glimpse of himself in the dresser mirror. "Ridiculous," he thought. "Who am I kidding?"

Then another unsettling thought presented itself. Cassandra! She would probably be there to watch the tryouts. His mood sank even lower as he made his way downstairs for breakfast.

The school day crawled by. At last the final bell rang, and it was time for the tryouts to begin. Sure enough, as Keagen and a handful of other unlikely hopefuls lined up outside the dugout, they were greeted by laughter and catcalls from the players who were already on the team and a number of students in the bleachers behind home plate. Franco led a few nasty chants, and many chimed in.

Only his promise to Baron kept Keagen from making a beeline for his bike and riding as far as it would go before the wheels fell off. He couldn't be sure, but he had the feeling Baron was nearby, watching. He straightened his back, pasted a smile on his face, and, pretending he didn't hear any of the remarks or laughter, walked directly up to Coach Willard, who was standing near the pitcher's mound.

"Well, well, well," Willard smirked, suppressing a cackle. "Look who's here. What a surprise."

Ignoring his remarks, Keagen lifted his chin as high as he could and said, "Coach, I would like to try out for the team."

"Why?" Willard's tone was unmistakable. Keagen felt he might as well have said, "*Go home, boy. You have no business here. We don't want you.*"

"I would like to play ball for the team this year."

"Sure, and I'd like to manage the New York Yankees," Willard sneered. "Not while I'm the coach, Keg-o."

"It's my right to at least try out," Keagen persisted, though his kneecaps were beginning to shake. He was afraid of Coach Willard, but he also hated him, and the bitterness and anger he felt as he met the man's gaze suddenly began to outweigh the fear.

"Your *right*, huh? Okay, fat Keg. Go ahead." The coach swept his arm out toward the field as if ushering Keagen to his doom. "But don't come cryin' for mama when you get hurt."

Keagen nodded and trotted out to take his assigned position in right field, thinking to himself, "Stupid, stupid, stupid! How stupid can I be?" He was more certain than ever this was going to end in disaster. All doubts were removed when he saw Coach Willard whispering to Franco and a few of the other "A" players.

He took a deep breath and repeated Baron's instructions to himself. "Give it your best shot. Try to have fun."

The tryouts went as expected, with Keagen taking beatings left and right. Players ran into him from all angles with unnecessary force, knocking him off his feet multiple times. When he was at bat, the pitcher repeatedly threw the ball at his body, and one pitch even struck him in the face, resulting in a bloody nose and black eye.

Watching from the stands, the spectators greeted several of the colossal hits Keagen took with collective "Ooohh's" and offered up loud boo's for the pitch in the face.

Despite the pummeling, Keagen managed to make almost as many catches as he missed in the field and, after striking out several times, got a base hit. He was positioned on third when the boy at bat popped a fly the left-fielder missed. Keagen charged toward home plate, trying hard to forget that the catcher was Franco.

The shortstop relayed the ball wildly, but Franco snagged it and proceeded to annihilate Keagen as he slid into home at full speed. It took Keagen almost a minute to get breath back into his lungs, then he waved his hands and said, "I'm okay." As he started for the dugout, however, he collapsed in pain, clutching his right foot, which Franco had thoroughly mangled in the play.

Gina, Waldo, and DiDi sat in the bleachers helplessly watching their friend get crushed. Gina kept up an almost constant monologue, talking more to herself than the other two. "Why is he doing this?" she said furiously, over and over. "I can't believe he would put himself in a position like this. What was he thinking? What is he trying to prove?"

Finally, she rammed her elbow sharply into Waldo's ribs, shouting, "Do something!"

"Ow!" Waldo bellowed. "Like what?"

When the ordeal was over, Coach Willard had the candidates stand along the third baseline. To everyone's surprise, Keagen dragged himself over to stand with the rest of the boys. Willard marched along in front of them like a boot camp drill instructor, clipboard in hand, blowing his whistle to silence the chatter on and off the field.

"Attention!" he said loudly enough for all to hear. "To everyone who tried out for the team, the school and I appreciate your efforts. We'd like to be able to pick more of you, but the reality is there's only room on the team for the most talented players. So, I've chosen only the best athletes, and to the rest of you, thanks and better luck next time. I'm now going to call out the names of the players who made the team. When you hear your name, step forward. If you do not hear your name, well . . . please go home."

"What a ridiculous, conceited monkey he is," Keagen thought. "Basking in the attention, so full of himself because he carries a stupid clipboard."

No one, least of all Keagen, was surprised when his name was not called. Many of the other boys who had been rejected departed the field with their heads down, sad and discouraged.

"Okay," Keagen thought to himself, sighing heavily. "Let me do this, and I hope Baron is watching so he'll be satisfied."

Bypassing Franco, Keagen walked up to the players who made the team, including some who had roughed him up during the tryouts. He extended his hand to each, offering congratulations. Most met his handshake with uncertainty and confused looks.

Finally, he approached Coach Willard and said, "Thank you, Coach. I appreciate your giving me the opportunity to be part of the tryouts. All the best to you and your team. I hope you have a great season. I'll cheer for you."

Without waiting for a response, Keagen turned and limped toward the locker room. He had no idea why, but he felt great—at least emotionally, for every bone in his body ached. As he walked past the bleachers toward the gym entrance, he heard a few people begin to clap. He looked into the stands and saw that more people were standing and applauding.

Keagen looked behind him toward the field, thinking maybe he had missed something, but he saw only Coach Willard and the chosen players still standing there, looking surprised. Turning back, he noticed the spectators were all looking at him, and then he heard his name, over and over. Slowly it dawned on him. People were cheering and *chanting his name*. Keagen stood staring blankly for a moment, then waved back weakly and continued hobbling toward the gym.

As he rounded the corner of the bleachers, one face in the crowd caught his eye. Cassandra was standing and cheering with the rest, her beautiful brown eyes sparkling, beaming a dazzling smile at him.

CHAPTER TEN

Standing Up for What's Right

"When did they start to get sick?" Keagen asked worriedly.
"From what we can tell, it began about six light-changes ago,"
Baron said, so concerned that he wasn't even aware he had given the
information in owl time. Keagen had arrived at the clearing in the middle of the summer afternoon to find the forest in an uproar.

"Three days," Keagen said. "Is it some kind of virus, like measles
or the flu in humans?"

"None of the owls is ill, and only a few other birds, mostly the
ducks," Baron reported. "A handful of deer, some of the foxes, almost
all of the otters, the beavers. The smaller species seem to be affected
most."

"Oh, Keagen, so many of the baby animals are sick," Salomona
said. In the months Keagen had spent with the owls, he had never seen
one cry, but he was sure he saw tears welling up in Salomona's eyes.
"They will die if we can't find a way to help them."

"This is weird. There has to be a reason for the outbreak. What
could be causing this?" Keagen wondered aloud. His heart was breaking as he thought of his animal friends suffering, but he tried to think
clearly. Though no one expected him to find a solution, he somehow
knew he could—in fact, that he might be their only chance.

"What else?" he thought, plopping down beside the little brook. As he watched the current gently sweep leaves and a few branches downstream, he noticed one or two dead fish as well. In fact, he remembered he had seen more dead fish in the stream over the past couple of weeks than in all the time he had been coming to the clearing. When Keagen mentioned his observation to Baron, the owl dismissed it as a periodic occurrence in the woodlands. Now Keagen wasn't so sure, and his heart began to race.

"The ducks, the otters, the beavers . . . the fish. The ones who are around the stream, in the stream, every day. Baron!" he finally shouted. "The water is bad. They must all stop drinking that water and swimming in the stream. It's poisoned!"

Keagen jumped to his feet and turned to his friend, who was perched on a low branch nearby. "I've got to see what's causing this. I'll walk upstream until I find out what's going on."

"I'll go with you, Keagen," Baron said. "You don't know that part of the woods."

"No, I'll be okay. You and the owls need to spread the word about the water." Keagen ran along the stream bank through the clearing and into the forest.

He followed the creek for almost two hours, picking his way as quickly as he could through the thick underbrush that grew beside it, crossing several times as the stream zigzagged around outcropped rocks and fallen tree trunks.

By now Keagen had lost all sense of direction. He had no idea where he was and had seen nothing that seemed wrong or out of place, though he wasn't at all sure what "out of place" might look like in a forest.

"Getting dark soon," he said to no one. He thought about turning back, retracing his steps to the clearing, and continuing the search the next day. But Salomona's words rang in his ears—how many of the animals might die if he waited?

He headed upstream again and soon reached a point where the water flow narrowed almost to a trickle. The creek bed turned up sharply to a small waterfall that splashed merrily down over a tall stack of boulders.

"Maybe a better view from up there," he thought, and scrambled up the side of the little cascade until he was standing on the highest of the rocks. The ground that sloped away before him looked soft and soggy. He could see water bubbling up from the ground in several places across the wet field. He had reached the stream's source.

Keagen took a step and felt mud ooze up around his shoes. After looking side to side for firmer footing, he finally chose a route to his right along the edge of the bog. Twenty yards on, he muttered, "This is leading nowhere," and was about to move back toward the waterfall when a small flash in the woods on the far side of the marshy area caught his eye. He continued picking his way gingerly across the soft earth until he was close enough to see that the shimmer of light came from the sun's fading rays reflecting on some sort of metal sign mired down in the mud.

Moving nearer, Keagen could see that someone had dug a shallow ditch where the woods picked up beyond the boggy field and then, apparently, covered it up again. Deep tire tracks led from the trench into the undergrowth. He frowned, then walked along the edge of the ditch until he reached the sign. It was affixed to a large metal barrel, and there were at least a dozen other identical containers next to it, some still buried in the mud, others partly exposed.

Keagen bent and wiped away the dirt on the sign. His breath caught, and he stepped back in disbelief. "No," he whispered. "No!"

He stared down at the gleaming silver logo of the company where his father worked, had worked for a couple of decades. Above it was the symbol for chemical waste, and below a series of letters, numbers and dashes. Keagen began to sob.

He pounded the drum with his fist and then carefully, intentionally memorized the code on the barrel. As he stood up, he heard his name being called from a distance away. It was Baron.

"Here!" Keagen shouted, waving.

Baron swooped down and landed on Keagen's outstretched arm. "Here it is," Keagen said sadly. "This is why they are sick, why they're dying."

"You must get back. It's almost dark," Baron replied. "Follow me and I'll show you a shorter return route. You can claim your bicycle tomorrow."

As Baron took off, Keagen leaped to his feet and began running after him into the woods. When they reached the road, Keagen waved and called, "Keep them away from the stream, Baron. I will get to the bottom of this."

It was well past dark when he stumbled through his front door. On the walk home, his anguish had hardened into rage, and he stormed up the stairs to his room without a word to anyone, even as his mother was calling, "Keagen! Keagen!" from the dining room.

He slammed the door and flung himself on his bed in the dark. In seconds his mother had thrown open the door and switched on the light. She now stood in the middle of his room with hands on hips, charged up like an electrical storm.

"Young man, where have you been?" she shouted. "You were supposed to be home over an hour ago. You are grounded for starters, and if you don't give me a reasonable explanation for your tardiness, your grounding will turn into a life sentence. Oh my God, look at you—covered in filth from top to bottom. Your sneakers are ruined! Your pants! I just washed those!" At this point his mother was fuming beyond reason. "Clean yourself up and come down to dinner. We will talk about this later." And poof, she was gone with a thundering slam of the door.

Keagen's hands were shaking. He was angry and anxious, and his mind was whirling at breakneck speed. He played out countless possible scenarios, hoping to come up with a reasonable explanation. But no matter how much he thought about it, he kept coming back to the same conclusion. The evidence did not lie. The person who was constantly reminding him he was not good enough . . . the person whose respect he most craved . . . his own father was—a murderer!

The family was still sitting at the dinner table when Keagen came downstairs. He sat hard on his chair and focused on his empty plate. His mother and sister stared at him and said nothing. His father was hidden behind the leftover pages of the morning newspaper.

"Keagen, where were you?" His mother finally broke the silence. Her voice was now quiet and concerned. "You know the rules. You have to be home before the streetlights come on. You were more than an hour late. Now, one more time, young man—where were you?"

"Investigating," Keagen snorted at her.

"What?"

"I was investigating a crime."

"Oh, brother," Sallie chimed in. "Now he thinks he's Sherlock Holmes."

"Shut up, Sallie! You have no idea what's going on!" Keagen snapped.

"What the heck are you talking about?" His sister rolled her eyes and threw a small bit of dinner roll onto Keagen's plate. He charged up out of his chair in fury.

"Quiet! Both of you!" his mother said. "Keagen, sit down. Sallie, I was talking to your brother. Please stay out of this. Again Keagen, where were you?"

"I just told you," he said through clenched teeth, his voice shaking. "I was investigating a murder case in the forest."

Sallie whooped, and his mother said, "The forest? You're telling me you were out in those woods until after dark? Have you lost your mind?"

By now even his father was paying attention. He lowered his newspaper and said, "Come on, Keagen. If you really were out in the forest all this time, what were you doing there? Tell your mother the truth and be done with it."

"The truth?" Keagen was screaming now. "Why don't *you* tell them the truth? Tell them how your company's dumping barrels of toxic crap in the forest—hiding them there—and poisoning the water. Animals are dying because of you! Go on—tell them!"

Keagen had jumped to his feet, knocking over his chair, his face flaming red. Everyone was staring in confusion. They had never seen him so angry. Other than occasional spats with Sallie, he rarely raised his voice, and never to either of his parents.

His father was particularly nonplussed. "I—I don't understand," he stammered.

"I saw them," Keagen went on, now almost in his father's face. "I saw them buried in the forest. That waste you and your company don't want anyone to know about. Why are you doing this? Why are you killing innocent creatures? They have families just like we do. Now their babies are sick, and some of the adults. You are killing them! I hate you!"

With tears running down his cheeks, Keagen charged back up to his room. He slammed the door and fell onto the bed, stifling his wracking sobs with his pillow.

After a few minutes, he moved to his desk, found a pencil and began sketching what he had seen: the barrels, the metal plate attached to the side of the container, the logo, and the serial number he had memorized.

There was a soft knock. He didn't answer, wishing desperately the world would just leave him alone. The door cracked open slowly, and his father's face appeared. Keagen couldn't remember the last time his father had been in his room.

"Keagen," his dad said, "may I come in?" The gentle tone was unexpected; Keagen had figured he was in for a strong reprimand, given how he had behaved at the table. Was this some sort of trick? Psychological warfare?

He nodded, and his father walked toward the extra chair at the foot of the bed, tossed the clothes and other items it held onto the floor, and sat down. "Look, Keagen," he began. "I don't know why you are so upset, or what happened to trigger this, but we're concerned about you. I, I mean we, have never seen you act like this. But whatever it was that set you off, you can't just yell and scream like a crazy person. You have to learn to express yourself with reason, and if something is bothering you, give others a chance to reflect and respond accordingly." He paused and then said, "Is this about the baseball tryouts? I told you I was sorry I couldn't be there . . . "

"This has nothing to do with the baseball tryouts!" Keagen's voice was rising again. "And I *did* tell you what was happening, but you didn't listen and you don't care! Nobody cares that whatever your stupid company is hiding in those barrels is killing the wildlife—*my friends*!"

"Keagen, I don't know anything about barrels hidden in the woods. Our plant doesn't dump harmful chemicals or anything else. The government has strict rules and guidelines that mandate a highly regulated protocol for how we seal, handle, and remove toxic waste, and we've abided by those regulations from the beginning without a breach. The EPA conducts unannounced inspections, and we always pass. I'm sorry you think your friends are in danger, whoever they are, but what you're accusing my company of just isn't true."

"Oh, yeah?" Keagen thrust his drawing into his father's face. "*This* is what I saw in the forest. *This* is what was on the side of those barrels."

His father stared at the picture in astonishment and said, "Where did you get this?"

"I just drew it."

"Where did you see this?" Alarm was rising in his father's voice.

"I told you," Keagen said in exasperation. "I found the barrels buried in the forest, about a mile or so up the little stream that flows under the bridge on the main highway. They're in a ditch where the stream starts, just a little ways from the east road. There were tire tracks leading up to them."

His father was now on his feet. "Do you have a flashlight?" Keagen nodded. "Get it. Do you think you can show me where those barrels are?" Keagen nodded again, and his father clambered down the stairs.

Keagen pulled a flashlight out of a drawer and went down to the front entry hall. He heard his father on the phone in the kitchen. His mother and sister were still sitting in the dining room with surprised looks on their faces.

"No," his father was saying. "There's no way Keagen could have known the serial number for the chemical waste. He definitely saw those barrels. Besides, I know my son, and he wouldn't lie. No question in my mind, and based on what he's telling me, they're near a water source, and they've started to leak. He says it's already affecting the wildlife. We have to act now. Okay . . . yes . . . you take care of contacting the EPA; I'll call the local authorities."

Keagen couldn't believe his ears. *I know my son, and he wouldn't lie?* Did his father actually just say that to his boss, or whoever was on the phone? He was stunned, elated, and relieved, all at the same time. It was clear to him that his father, and from the sound of it, the company he worked for, had no knowledge of the barrels in the woods.

His dad hung up and dialed again, this time connecting with the sheriff's office. After briefly describing the dangerous nature of the chemical waste inside the containers and the urgency of the situation, he said, "Yes. Keagen knows where they are. We'll wait here at the house until you come pick us up in the squad car." He paused, listening. "Our president, Don Samuelson, is on his way over as well, and he's in touch with the EPA. Once we find the barrels, we'll notify the agency of the location so they can get the cleanup under way." He listened again, and all the blood drained from his face.

"Keagen," his father said, voice shaking. "Did you touch any of those barrels or have any contact with what was in them?"

"Not really, Dad. I wiped the dirt off the side of one of them, and I walked around in the mud where they were," he said.

His father spoke into the phone again. "No, Officer, he says he didn't . . . Yes, I think that's a wise idea. We'll stop by the hospital after he leads us to the site . . . I know . . . I'm aware of the danger."

Keagen's eyes widened at this. His father hung up the phone and walked over to him, placing his hands on the boy's shoulders. "You're sure none of the toxic solution in those containers touched your skin or clothes?" he said.

"I—I don't think so. Just my shoes, maybe, if any of the stuff was in the mud where they were buried," Keagen said. Without another word, his father took Keagen into his arms and held him tight. Keagen swallowed hard and hugged him back. "Thank God," his dad whispered.

"Todd?" By now his mother had come into the kitchen, with Sallie right behind. "What on earth is going on?"

"Dad," Keagen mumbled, still a little stunned by his father's unexpected embrace. "You really didn't know anything about this, did you?"

"No, Keagen," his father replied. "I didn't know, and neither did anyone at my company. But thanks to you, we're going to stop the people responsible." He paused. All three of them were looking at him expectantly. "You see," he continued, "we use an outside company to remove and recycle the waste produced in our manufacturing processes. They're supposed to be experts, EPA-certified to dispose of the harmful materials safely. A couple of months ago, we started using a new contractor for this. Looks like someone on their payroll found a way to cut costs and increase profit by just dumping the waste in the woods. At least, that's what we suspect."

He cleared his throat and stared at the floor. "The toxins are so potent, they could contaminate the groundwater for miles around. If they get into the town's water supply, a lot of people could get very sick." Now he looked directly at Keagen. "I'm so sorry about the animals. Mr. Samuelson was calling the Department of Natural Resources as well as the EPA. They'll do whatever they can for them."

There was a knock on the front door. His father answered and ushered his boss into the living room, where they spoke in quiet voices. Keagen could see lights flashing outside the house as the sheriff's patrol car pulled into the driveway. "Let's go," his father said.

The aftermath of the eventful evening forever changed life in the forest, and Keagen's as well. He read in the newspapers that the company responsible for dumping the toxins had closed down, and several of its executives and employees were arrested and charged. Both he and his father were mentioned as heroes for uncovering the crime in time to prevent contamination of the city's water system, but Keagen didn't care. He had been too late for the beaver and otter babies and a number of other animals who lost their fight with the sickness caused by the poisons in the stream. He was heartbroken and didn't feel heroic in the least, no matter what the papers wrote about him.

After the barrels were removed, heavy construction machinery was brought in to bulldoze the site and haul away the toxic earth. The water in the little stream was tested and re-tested and finally declared safe once again for wildlife.

Baron, his family, and most of the other animals relocated to the woods near Silver Lake, whose waters were fed by a different spring. It was more than six month before they were able to return to Owls' Meadow. Keagen's brave acts were acknowledged in the forest with a mix of gratitude and sorrow, and his bond with Baron grew deeper.

CHAPTER ELEVEN

Arondight

The only impeccable place in Keagen's room was a four-foot-long hanging shelf over his desk. In the center sat a carefully displayed, 1/48 scale model of *Arondight*, the greatest and fastest racing yacht ever to sail the Seven Seas.

Keagen had received the kit for his tenth birthday, which stood out as, up to that point, the best day of his life. The model was simple, made of prefabricated plastic parts that required only a bit of glue to put together and some paint to finish, but it took him three months to complete the project. Keagen was determined his work would be perfect, and it was just that. The model was his masterpiece, meticulously assembled and articulated with great love and care.

The shelf was surrounded by colorful posters of the boat and pencil sketches Keagen had copied from photographs of the yacht at sea. Her presence was breathtaking. The sleek, snow-white hull extended a graceful 180 feet from bow to stern, creating 215 tons of displacement. The two main masts reached more than 90 feet into the sky, and her foremast pointed ahead at a sharp angle, boldly signaling to the oceans who truly ruled. All three sails were bright red, and, at full capacity, challenged the winds with almost 19,700 square feet of near-indestructible canvas, catapulting her through the water at an exhilarating top speed of sixteen knots.

For a vessel of such beauty and majesty, no ordinary name would do, and hers was perfect: *Arondight*, after the powerful, mystical sword carried by the legendary Sir Lancelot du Lac of King Arthur's Round Table.

The shelf and its contents were Keagen's holy grail, his shrine of dreams. Through it, he could escape into a world of freedom and unlimited adventure, in which he was strong and confident, and where he mattered.

Often as he sat at his desk, attempting to complete his homework, he would stare at the posters until he became lost in his imagination, envisioning himself at the yacht's helm. In these moments, the *Arondight* transformed from a vision born in slumber to one that kept him awake. He was a man and his boat, conquering the mighty seas.

With her sails trimmed and ready to catch the winds, he grasps her silver-plated wheel with both hands and senses the pure energy and strength coursing through the hull, waiting to be unleashed on the open ocean. He leans her into the wind and says, "Come on, my girl, let's chase the sun!"

He hears her sails billow overhead as she slices through the water in all her glory. He feels the spray of the ocean on his face, the sting on his skin and the smell of the salt air. He is connected with the very core of the craft's existence, confronting the sea with every wave and celebrating this perfect moment for which she was created.

His visions were usually interrupted at this point by a knock on the door or a loud shout from his mother in the kitchen. "Keagen! Dinner is ready! Wash your hands and come downstairs."

It always took Keagen a few minutes to recover from the jarring shipwreck of return to reality. Snapping back from one of his sailing adventures, he had to let his pulse get back to normal and sometimes wipe beads of sweat from his forehead. And every time, he thought to himself, "One day, *one day*, I'll own her. One day I will set sail and discover the world."

The only other item allowed on the shelf with the model of the *Arondight* was a three-foot cardboard tube propped lengthwise against the wall behind the tiny replica. It represented his first step in making the dream come true.

Keagen knew there were only two actual *Arondight*s still in existence, and he thought it unlikely he would ever be able to purchase one of them. So, he had come up with a Plan B. When the time was right, he solemnly pledged, he would build a version of her himself from scratch.

Touching every part of the magnificent boat, he would ultimately become the creator that gave her life. He read countless books about shipbuilding from the local library. Some of these included unreadable copies of blueprints and comments from craftsmen who had helped build an *Arondight*, but Keagen couldn't locate a source for the boat's actual design specifications. He would have to improvise and create these himself, he decided, based on what he had read.

That brought him to his next stopping point. Keagen had the basic drawing tools, but he needed proper architect's blueprint and tracing paper, for which he had neither the money nor the access. Discouraged, he put his dream project on hold.

On a rainy fall day near the beginning of his last year of middle school, Keagen volunteered to spend his study hall period tidying up and organizing the supply closet adjacent to the school's art room for Mrs. Stockton.

He had climbed up a small stepladder and was moving some boxes on one of the higher shelves when suddenly he froze. There before him were four cardboard storage tubes, each clearly marked "Blueprint." He opened one of the tubes and partially pulled out the roll of unused blueprint paper and sheets of translucent tracing paper inside. His hands trembled and his heart started pounding in his throat. This was his chance—Mrs. Stockton must have had the material left over from a past class project. And now here it was, waiting for him to use!

He finished straightening the shelf and then tucked one of the tubes under his arm and climbed down from the ladder. Though his guilt about taking the paper was somewhat offset by his excitement that he could finally get started on his very own *Arondight*, he began rationalizing furiously. "That paper was extra—Mrs. Stockton didn't need it for her class," he said to himself. "It's just been sitting there, who knows how long. She'll never miss just one roll. Besides, it was meant to be. Why else would I have just happened to be cleaning the storage closet and see those tubes? It's for a greater cause."

He slipped quietly through the empty art room and deposited the cardboard tube in his locker. That afternoon, he waited until he was sure all the teachers and students had left the school building and retrieved the purloined paper, bicycling home as fast as he could. Safe in his room, he peeked at the thick, light-sensitive blueprint roll and withdrew the sheets of architect's tracing paper. He was ready to begin the process of bringing *Arondight* to life.

At the library, he found fairly detailed blueprints and specification drawings of other sailing vessels with similar dimensions and modified these, detail by detail, to recreate the *Arondight*'s design. It took him most of the school year, but when he was done, the cardboard tube held more than thirty spec sheets and sketches, as accurate and professionally drawn as his by now fourteen-year-old mind and hands could render. He nestled the tube in a place of honor on the shelf just behind his plastic model. The next step would be to begin actually building her!

Keagen was proud of his work. He showed the drawings to DiDi, Waldo, and Gina, who he felt didn't truly appreciate the enormity of what he had done. He longed for a more public audience for his accomplishment, and the opportunity came about in a most unexpected way.

English class under Miss Nepita was this year's least-favorite subject for Keagen, due primarily to the teacher's sarcastic criticism of his work and biting comments about Keagen's level of academic intelligence. He hated the various writing assignments, but near the end of the school year, Miss Nepita introduced a project that made his heart leap with joy. Each class member was to choose an item of importance in his or her life—a photograph, book, hobby, even a pet—and write an essay about the item's significance. Then, the students would bring the objects to class and read their respective essays. This was Keagen's chance to share the greatest story of his life. He would introduce the world to his *Arondight*.

His presentation at first went surprisingly well. He displayed his model, along with the blueprint specifications and renderings of the yacht, which Miss Nepita made clear she did not believe Keagen had drawn himself. He then read his essay, concluding with his plan to build the sailboat himself from the ground up. At this, Miss Nepita let out a sharp "Ha!" adding, "Oh, *really*?", and the class joined in her laughter.

Keagen didn't care. They wouldn't understand anyway. He had begun to wrap up his speech when he heard a gentle, familiar voice at the classroom door say, "Miss Nepita, I'm sorry to interrupt, but could I make an announcement to your class?"

It was Mrs. Stockton, the last person in the world Keagen either expected or wanted to see at that moment. He was unable to move, caught holding one of the renderings fully unfurled on the blueprint material he had taken from the art supply room. The paper now seemed almost to burn his fingertips.

"Of course, Mrs. Stockton," Miss Nepita said. "Come in. Keagen is just finishing his presentation."

Mrs. Stockton reminded anyone who was in her art class to bring aprons or old clothes to wear for the oil painting class she had scheduled for the next day. She then looked straight at Keagen, who was still standing frozen at the front of the classroom, staring at his drawings as if they were radioactive.

"My, what have we here?" she asked.

Miss Nepita shared briefly about the essay assignment, raising her eyebrows as she explained that Keagen had made a presentation "about 'the greatest sailing yacht of all time.' He claims to have drawn these blueprints himself," she said. Then, giggling, she added, "Oh, and I forgot to mention that he intends to use these plans to actually *build* the boat. Soon, apparently!"

The class chimed in with another round of laughter.

Mrs. Stockton walked closer to examine the blueprints, then looked at Keagen. He could feel the heat as his face flushed. She looked again at the drawings and back at him. "Oh no—*busted!*" was all he could think.

"Don't mind them," Mrs. Stockton said, pointedly enough that the class quieted down. "These are very well-drawn—in fact, they look quite professional. Excellent job, Keagen." She turned and walked out.

Keagen was finally able to breathe again. Could he possibly be so lucky that Mrs. Stockton didn't wonder where he got the paper? Had she not put two and two together and realized it was *her* blueprint paper?

By the time he sat down in study hall for the last period of the day, he had almost forgotten he'd nearly been caught red-handed. As the bell rang for school to be out, however, he saw Mrs. Jones, the school administrative assistant, standing at the study hall door, motioning to him.

"Mrs. Stockton wants to see you in her classroom before you leave today. What did you do now?" she snarled. "You just can't stay out of trouble, can you? Anyway, she said for you to 'bring the draw-ings,' whatever that means. Hurry up, don't keep the teacher waiting."

His heart sank like a stone. "How could I be so stupid?" he thought. "I should never have brought those plans to school." Worst of all was the fact that Mrs. Stockton was the only teacher he really liked, the only one who was nice to him. Now he had disappointed her, betraying her kindness. He was embarrassed and ashamed.

Keagen stopped by his locker to collect the drawings, then walked slowly to the art room. He knocked and heard a soft, "Come in, please."

Mrs. Stockton was reading, peering through small, round glasses perched at the very tip of her nose. Looking up, she said, "Hello, Keagen. Please have a seat." Her tone of voice was pleasant, and her eyes sparkled with kindness, which confused him. Pinched by guilt, he flopped down into a desk directly in front of her, drop-ping his book bag to the floor.

"That's very good work you did there," she said, nodding toward the drawings Keagen held tightly across his lap. "Did you really draw all those by yourself?"

"Yes," he said, sounding a bit too loud and defensive. "Yes, I did," he said again, much softer.

"And nobody helped you? Maybe your father?"

"My dad?" he said, puzzled, thinking, "Help me? My dad can't even pronounce the word *Arondight*." To Mrs. Stockton he said, "No, ma'am. I drew them myself."

"May I see them again, please?" she asked kindly.

He popped the round metal lid from the cardboard tube and, hands shaking, pulled out the roll of blueprints. Mrs. Stockton made room on her desk by sliding papers and other items to either side, like a swimmer doing the breaststroke. She then rolled open the drawings and reviewed each one carefully.

After a few minutes, she said, "How?"

Keagen wasn't at all sure to what she was referring. How did he steal the blueprint paper? Or how was he able to smuggle it out of the school building? "Ma'am?" he asked.

"How did you draw these without assistance? Without instruction?" she said.

"Oh," he replied. "Well, I did have some help. I used some ship-building books from the city library. I couldn't find actual specifications for *Arondight*, but there were plenty of blueprints and information from other sailboats sort of like her. I used those designs as an outline and changed their specs to match what I'd read about her size and dimensions and design."

"Remarkable," she mumbled under her breath, flipping through the sheets again. "Truly remarkable indeed." She suddenly leveled a gaze at him with eyes as cold as ice, and he knew what was coming next.

"You took the blueprint paper out of the art supply room, didn't you?" she said.

Keagen's stomach turned into a giant knot. He stared at the floor, unable to speak at all, and slowly nodded his head.

"You know that's stealing."

Keagen nodded again.

"Please look at me when I speak to you," she said firmly.

When he finally raised his eyes to hers, he had to look away again at once. "I'm so sorry," he choked out. "I thought it was just scraps, that nobody would need it."

"Ah, no excuses, Keagen. The very least you can do is take responsibility for your crime."

He looked up in surprise. He knew it was wrong to take the paper, but . . . a crime?

"I didn't mean to," he lied. Then again, "I'm so sorry."

"Why didn't you just ask me for the paper?" she pressed. "I would have given it to you."

"I didn't have any money."

"I did not say that I would have sold the paper to you. I said I would have given it to you. As a gift, to support your project."

His mind was now in a whirl, and he felt tears welling up in his eyes. He shrugged his shoulders and shook his head. "I . . . I don't really know why I took it, ma'am. I guess I just thought I needed it."

"Well, Keagen," Mrs. Stockton said after a few moments. "It seems we have ourselves a big problem. Stealing is stealing, no matter the cause. I was looking for the blueprint paper not too long ago, and I knew exactly where I had put it. I thought I was a roll short, and I even asked Mr. Sonders, the school's maintenance engineer, if he might have thrown out one of the tubes by mistake. You see, I got the paper from a friend of mine who is an architect. His firm's initials are at the bottom of each sheet. Imagine my surprise when I recognized those initials this morning on your drawings."

Keagean squeezed his eyes shut. He had thought the initials were of the company that manufactured the paper.

"So," she continued, "what are we going to do about this mess? If I report the theft to Principal Alston, you will be suspended, possibly even expelled. And, of course, I will need to speak with your parents."

The words rang in Keagen's ears like a death sentence, and Mrs. Stockton saw with satisfaction the terror on his face.

She let her comments sink in for a few minutes. Keagen finally broke the silence as he started to cry and begged, "Please, Mrs. Stockton, I'll do anything, but please don't tell my parents. Please!"

She continued to look at him unflinchingly. "I will consider your request, but this act cannot go unpunished. I have a proposition for you. I am willing to give you a chance to redeem yourself, but you must do exactly as I ask, with no resistance and no complaints."

Surprise and the slim possibility of a reprieve brightened Keagen's expression. Mrs. Stockton continued, "A friend of mine, Mr.

Otto Jürgen, is a master carpenter who owns a woodworking and cabinetry store in town. Do you know him?"

"No ma'am, I don't think so," he replied.

"Good," she said, "because you *will* get to know him. He and his staff create expertly crafted, custom items in the shop behind his store, and the woodworking machines make quite a mess. He is currently in need of someone to clean the floors and keep the workplace in neat condition. You will fill that position. You are to complete thirty-six work hours, six per day, over the next six Saturdays without incident, assisting Mr. Jürgen with whatever he needs done in his shop. It's hard work, and he expects a lot of his employees, so this will not be an easy job. You must be on time and perform the tasks you are assigned impeccably.

"If I get good reports on your performance, I am willing to forgive this incident about the blueprint paper—no one else shall ever know," she continued. "However, if you are late even once, or if I learn from Mr. Jürgen that you are lazy or do incomplete work or talk back to those in charge, this deal is off, and we will immediately hold a meeting with your parents and Principal Alston. Do I make myself clear?"

"Yes, ma'am," Keagen replied quickly and meekly, relief washing over him.

"One more thing," she said. "Your *Arondight* blueprints stay with me until you have completed your punishment. You need to remember what you are working for, and in case you fail, I'll need them as evidence."

Keagen swallowed hard. He hated the thought of being separated from his most prized possession, but what choice did he have? He nodded. Mrs. Stockton rolled the papers back up neatly, placed them into the cardboard tube and snapped the lid closed.

"You can go now, Keagen. Please tell your parents you have this job, though as I said you do not have to tell them the circumstances through which you got it. Have them call me if they have any questions, and I promise to keep our agreement. You'll need to report to Mr. Jürgen this coming Saturday morning at 9:00 a.m. sharp. He is expecting you. Do you know where his store is located?"

"I'll find it," Keagen answered, sliding out of the desk and walking to the door. Before he reached for the handle, he turned back and said, "Mrs. Stockton, thank you. I really am sorry." She nodded and waved him out, waiting until he was gone to allow herself a satisfied smile.

Later that afternoon, Keagen confessed to Baron about the incident and his penance. His friend jumped up and down on the tree limb where he was perched and almost shouted, "Bravo, Mrs. Stockton! Well done!"

Keagen was shocked at his reaction. "Wait a minute! I thought you were on my side!" he thundered back.

"My dear boy, I am most certainly on your side." Baron fluffed up, then smoothed down his feathers. "Mrs. Stockton is doing you a big favor, Keagen, by teaching you a valuable lesson. Stealing is a crime. Beyond that, it is a total betrayal of the person you are, of your morals and values, and you know it. Besides which, can you imagine how all this would have been if the teacher were Mr. Heldrich or Miss Nepita? You would have been cooked . . . twice. First at school, then at home. Mrs. Stockton is truly your friend."

"I know, *I know*," Keagen said. "But still . . . "

"But still what?"

"I won't be able to hang out with you on Saturdays for the next six weeks," Keagan said sadly.

"Worse things can happen. The time will go by faster than you think." Baron paused, furrowing the feathers on his brow. "Speaking of spending time, have you been 'hanging out,' as you say, with your friends lately?"

"Some."

"You know," Baron continued, "I truly enjoy having you visit with us here in the forest, Keagen. It's always a pleasure being with you. But you must not overlook your friends nor neglect your obligations in order to spend time with me and the other owls. It's not how much time we are together but rather the quality of the time when we see each other that counts. I understand you are a busy young man. Your life is getting bigger every day. I will not be sad or hurt or angry if you can't always come here and 'hang out.'"

"What are you saying, Baron? Don't you like me coming around?" He looked stricken.

Baron sighed. "Please listen carefully to me, Keagen. We all love you. We love for you to come here. But we also know you are part of a world beyond this forest, and it's time you began expanding how you participate in that world. It's an important part of your growing up. Does that make sense?"

"I guess so," Keagen said, still dejected.

"My, you are so sensitive," Baron said, clucking his tongue in his beak. "Keagen, do you understand what constructive criticism is?"

"It's when somebody tells you something they think is for your own good, but it makes you mad."

Baron laughed. "Not everything you don't like to hear is directed against you or intended to make you angry. Taking advice and constructive criticism more positively is a valuable skill that will serve you well all your life. You must learn to tell the difference between people who are being critical of you for their own reasons and those who are offering advice and suggestions because they care about you and want you to succeed."

He paused to make sure Keagen was paying attention. "If you surround yourself only with people who say nice things and tell you what you want to hear, you will never learn, or grow, or improve. They may see you make mistakes, but they will keep their mouths shut. Do you think they are interested in your personal development? Not all criticism is uncalled for. You want friends who will point out your shortcomings at times, with kindness, and you should not be so sensitive when they do so.

"I am one of those who care about you, Keagen, and I am telling you—spend more time with your friends. They are loyal comrades, and these are wonderful, magical days that you will never get back. I advise you to live them wisely."

"Okay, *okay*! Don't get your feathers in a clip," Keagen snapped. He seldom smarted off to his friend, and he immediately felt bad about it. "I'm sorry, Baron. I—I have to go."

The owl sat quietly, watching the boy push his bike down the path into the woods. "I still have a long way to go with you, my young friend, but you are worth it," he whispered. "You are worth every minute of my time."

At school the next day, Keagen sheepishly told Gina, Waldo, and DiDi about the theft and his "prison sentence" working at Jürgen's shop. "So, I guess my weekends, at least my Saturdays, are out of commission for a while," he concluded.

Gina was indignant. "I can't believe you stole that paper from Mrs. Stockton. I thought you were a better person than that, Keagen."

"So did she," Keagen sighed. "But I really am sorry, and now I will be paying for my crime."

Waldo and DiDi could barely contain their glee that Keagen had been collared in the middle of his presentation, and Keagen almost blurted out that Baron also approved of Mrs. Stockton's arrest and retribution. DiDi had told the group about the injured "pet owl" Keagen had found and nursed back to health, but none of the friends knew about his ability to communicate with Baron and his family. The owls had become so much a part of Keagen's life it was difficult to keep his unique relationship with them a secret.

"What are you telling your parents?" Gina asked.

"That it's a school-related project," Keagen replied, with a sick grin on his face. "Which is the truth—but not the whole truth."

"And they buy that?" Waldo chimed in.

"So far, no issues and no questions," Keagen said. "My dad even gave me a pat on the shoulder."

"Well, we'll probably be at the Treehouse a lot on the weekends. If you have time, stop on by," DiDi said.

"Great!" Keagan said brightly, adding, "I meant to tell you guys that I'm sorry I haven't been around much lately. Got busy with stuff, you know, but I want to change that. I miss hanging out with you. I'll stop by on Sundays, or after I'm done at the shop on Saturdays."

The three friends exchanged bemused looks. This was the old Keagen back in their midst. "Okay, Keg, whatever you say," Waldo said finally, confused but pleased.

"Waldo!" Gina barked, her face turning red. "It's Keagen. His name is Keagen." She spoke as if Keagen weren't standing next to her. "When will that finally become clear in your hollow brain?"

Waldo just grinned at her, always amused and even impressed by the way she consistently stood up for each of them.

"Come on, guys," DiDi said. "Class is about to start. No need to fuel Miss Nepita's fire by walking in late."

CHAPTER TWELVE

Jürgen's Shop

Saturday arrived almost before Keagen knew it. He found himself standing in front of Otto Jürgen's shop promptly at 8:55 a.m., ready to begin his mandatory employment.

The small storefront was nestled beneath a large, ornately carved sign that read, "Jürgen's Woodworking—Fine Cabinets & Furniture." Keagen was staring up at the imposing marquee when a tall, equally imposing man stepped through the door.

"Ah," Mr. Jürgen said, walking up to him. "You must be Keagen. I have heard much about you." He didn't smile or offer his hand to shake.

"Yes, uh . . . ," Keagen mumbled shyly.

"You mean, 'Yes, Mr. Jürgen.'"

"Yes, sir, Mr. Jürgen," Keagan repeated, clearer and a bit bolder.

"Mrs. Stockton shared with me what you did, and that to make up for it you are assigned to help me around the store over the next six Saturdays. So . . . I have some rules, and you had better listen carefully."

"Yes, Mr. Jürgen," Keagen stuttered back.

"Come in, and I'll give you a work shirt. Don't have any trousers that small. Can you get those pants dirty?"

"I guess so," Keagen answered.

"What does *that* mean?" Mr. Jürgen said sharply. "I asked you a straight, yes-or-no question, and I expect a straight, yes-or-no answer."

"Yes, Mr. Jürgen," Keagen said, feeling his knees begin to shake.

"All right, then. Why did you not say so? Speak up when you talk to me."

Jürgen was in his mid-thirties, and at six feet, four inches, towered over Keagen. He was built like a prizefighter, with upper arms easily as big around as Keagen's thighs and covered with tattoos. He had earrings in both ears and no hair, which made his long, pointed nose look even more so.

Keagen at first thought he detected kindness in the man's incredibly dark eyes, but that idea went out the window once he started to speak. His deep, powerful voice was as intimidating as his appearance. "Oh, man," Keagen thought, "this is truly going to be hell. I hope I survive in one piece."

He donned the rumpled but clean chambray work shirt Mr. Jürgen tossed him. It was two sizes too large, and Keagen rolled up the sleeves that extended well past his hands, feeling he looked like a toddler dressed up in his father's clothes.

"The Rules," Mr. Jürgen said authoritatively. "These are the conditions for working in this shop. I will report to Mrs. Stockton immediately if you violate any of them. Clear?"

"Yes, Mr. Jürgen."

Jürgen scrutinized him critically, then continued. "First, be on time. Arriving five minutes before your shift begins is considered late. No excuses. That means you were late today, but I'm giving you a break because you did not know The Rules yet. You will report here every Saturday no later than 8:54 a.m. sharp for six hours of work, and you will do that for the next six weekends straight. If you have any conflicts because of family obligations, I need to know now, so that we can reschedule.

"Next," he went on. "You will do as I tell you. If you have any questions, speak up immediately. Don't wait until later when I find out you have screwed something up, and you give me excuses like you didn't understand the orders. You will tell me as soon as you've completed a task, and I'll inspect to see if I'm satisfied with the work.

"Third, don't lift anything that is too heavy. Ask me, Tim, or Dirk to help you. I can't afford having to send you to the hospital and pay some expensive workman's comp claim. That goes for the wood-working machines, too. You are only permitted to touch or clean them when I specifically tell you to. Never touch a machine that is running or in motion. Clear?"

"Yes, sir."

"If you break something, tell me. I will kill you quickly. I promise."

Jürgen saw the blood drain from Keagen's face and chuckled. "Relax, boy. That was a joke. Mrs. Stockton must have forgotten to tell you I have a wicked sense of humor."

Keagen exhaled with relief, thinking, "'Wicked' doesn't begin to cover it."

"And the last Rule," Jürgen concluded. "Don't ask me when you have to take a leak. Just go and come back quickly. If you take more than three breaks an hour, though, you will have to deal with me, and it's not going to be pretty. Got it? Any questions? Good, then. Get started already. This is not a charitable organization. We work for a living here."

Keagen was given a wide variety of tasks to perform on his first day, none of them difficult but all somewhat physically demanding, from sweeping and stacking boxes to cleaning a few windows.

As ordered, he checked in with Mr. Jürgen after completing each assignment and received a brisk nod, which Keagen took for approval since the man's face was almost impossible to read. Pedaling his bike back home, he could feel every muscle in his body aching.

Keagen dragged himself into the kitchen and opened the icebox. As he reached for the milk bottle to pour a cold glass, he saw four cuts of meat sitting neatly on a platter, covered with plastic wrap. His mother was probably planning to have his father grill them for dinner that night.

"Perfect," he thought. "Just what I need." He took the largest filet and placed it on the knot on his forehead where he had bumped into a board jutting out from a stack of lumber in the workshop. Then he moved the slab of beef to his neck, his shoulders and finally his lower back. The cool, soft texture of the meat was soothing and eased the muscle pain a bit. His mother's voice interrupted the healing process, and Keagen quickly replaced the steak on the platter in the fridge as she walked toward him.

"How was the school work project today?" she asked.

"Fine," he replied, a little too hastily. "I'm going upstairs to take a shower."

"What happened to you?" Sallie snorted when she noticed Keagen moving somewhat stiffly toward the dinner table that evening. "Ballet class really tough today?"

Keagen ignored her, smiling with satisfaction when she grabbed the largest grilled filet for herself. "Hey, Sis," he smirked, after she had savored several juicy bites. "How are you enjoying that steak?"

She gave him a puzzled look. Keagen said nothing more but couldn't help chuckling with every morsel she devoured.

The next day, he rode his bike to the Treehouse to meet up with the gang.

"Hey, Keg!" Waldo greeted him with an excited smile. Gina hadn't yet arrived, so he knew he was safe from an elbow to the ribs at the use of Keagen's nickname.

"What's up, guys?" Keagen said cheerfully, realizing suddenly how much he had missed their company over the past few months.

"How was the first day on the job?" DiDi asked.

"Okay, I guess. I mean, it's hard work, and Jürgen is not anybody to joke with, but it could be worse."

"So, what do you have to do?" Waldo asked. "Six hours is a long time. I can't imagine working that many hours in a day. That's just not right."

"You can say that again," Keagen agreed. "My arms and feet are killing me."

"So what does he make you do?" DiDi repeated Waldo's question.

Keagen lowered his voice to add significance to his reply. "Cleaning mostly. Doing the dirty work."

His friends continued to look at him expectantly.

"Organize shelves, sweep the floor, wipe door frames, refill the water supply, restock the lumber outside, clean the break room. Stuff like that," Keagen explained. "It's a small carpentry factory, and sawdust can cover the floor a foot high when the machines are running. I have to sweep, put the wood shavings into big bags, and take them to the dumpster."

"That sounds awful," said Waldo. "Do they treat you all right?"

"Jürgen's two employees, Dirk and Tim, are kind of jerks. They played a practical joke on me yesterday, and Jürgen jumped all over them. Now I think they'll pretty much leave me alone. Jürgen is tough—nobody crosses him. But as long as I do what he's asked me to do, he doesn't bother me."

"What practical joke?" Waldo asked.

"Never mind," Keagen replied.

"Come on. Tell us," Waldo pressed.

"I'd rather not."

"Why?" It was DiDi's turn to query.

"Because it just wasn't funny, that's why," Keagen snapped, ending the conversation.

The humiliation of Dirk's and Tim's prank still rankled Keagen. Both were in their twenties. Dirk attended the local university in the evenings, and Tim, who was several years older, clearly was Jürgen's right-hand man. The previous afternoon, Dirk and Tim had approached Keagen in a state of panic. They had forgotten to pick up the woodchip-splitting machine Jürgen was borrowing from another shop for an important project he planned to begin on Monday. The boss was away at a client lunch but would be back in just over an hour. He would be furious, they said, if the machine was not there when he returned. The two of them had to stay and man the store; Keagen would need to rush to the other shop to retrieve it.

He wouldn't be able to take his bike, they explained, as the box containing the machine was large and so heavy he would have to carry it with both arms. Tim confirmed the other shop was expecting Keagen to pick it up right away. He would have to run to make it.

And run he did, as fast as he could, for almost a mile. He raced into the other shop entirely out of breath, and an employee there pointed him toward a big, sealed box on a worktable. The equipment was fragile, he was told. He would have to be extra-cautious carrying it, taking care not to tilt it or set it down, and he must not, under any circumstances, drop it.

The box became heavier with each step. It took all his strength to make it back to Jürgen's shop, and his arm and back muscles were screaming as he gently lowered the box onto a table in the workshop.

Tim and Dirk were working at the wood-drilling bench, and Dirk nodded approvingly at Keagen. Minutes later, Mr. Jürgen strode through the door from the store to the workshop. Still a bit out of breath, Keagen announced proudly that he had fetched the woodchip-splitting machine from Dobson's Cabinets downtown. At that moment he heard Tim and Dirk explode into laughter, doubling over and holding their stomachs. Dirk finally stumbled over to the table, grabbed a box-cutter and sliced open the sealed container, which was filled to the top with nothing but scrap wood.

Keagen felt his face go from hot to scorching red. They were all in on the stupid newbie joke, and he had fallen for it completely! "Keagen the Loser," he thought miserably. "Nothing's changed."

Though Jürgen scolded both boys for the prank, he, too, joined in the laughter. He gave Keagen a hearty slap on the back. "We've all been the new kid, my boy," he chuckled. "Don't take it personally. A sense of humor is life's greatest gift."

Keagen's silent recollection was interrupted as Gina pushed her bike over the little hill to the lake and shouted enthusiastically, "Keagen! It's so great to see you!" She climbed up the ladder to the Treehouse and sat down beside him. "How is the job?"

"Hard," he replied.

"Tell me about it," she said.

"Just did. You missed it."

"Hmm . . . that bad?"

"No, not really." Keagen paused thoughtfully. "Lots of sweeping and picking things up, but there are a few neat things I get to see, too."

"Like what?"

"Mr. Jürgen is a true master with wood. He does stuff nobody else can even come close to. He works on the complicated stuff, custom work that requires real precision. It's incredible to watch him on those machines. The guy is good—the best there is, apparently. He showed me a few things and stressed how important it is to be detailed in every aspect."

Keagen's enthusiasm took over at this point. "He says everything is in the planning. Once he starts the work, it has to be precise and accurate. If he is off by even one millimeter, the whole project is a failure, and he has to start all over again. Of course, I'm not allowed to speak to him or disturb him when he is using the machines, but he lets me watch him work the wood. He made a custom cabinet yesterday that looked amazing. All the details came together and fit like a glove."

"Cool," Gina said. "How many more Saturdays will you be working there?"

"Five."

"Well, it'll be over before you know it," she said encouragingly.

The late spring weather was fairly warm, and the four friends spent the rest of the afternoon swimming and leaping from the Treehouse tire swing into the refreshing waters of the lake.

Gina's prediction proved correct. The remaining Saturdays at Jürgen's shop came and went quickly for Keagen. On his last day, he cleaned the work areas and completed the tasks he was assigned, as always. He was anxious to get Mr. Jürgen's final evaluation and learn what he planned to report to Mrs. Stockton. She was holding Keagen's most prized possessions hostage, and he wanted them back, badly. He finished his last hour, then went to the locker room to hang up his work shirt. When he walked back into the shop, Mr. Jürgen was standing with Tim and Dirk around the large main worktable.

"So," Mr. Jürgen said, somewhat mysteriously. "Sentence completed, huh?"

"Yes, Mr. Jürgen," Keagen replied. And he couldn't help exhaling with relief and satisfaction.

"How do you think you did?" Jürgen asked bluntly.

"Okay, I hope," Keagen replied.

Turning to Tim and Dirk, Mr. Jürgen repeated the question. "What do you think, boys? Did he do okay?"

Tim spoke first, sounding uncertain and critical. "Well, I'm not so sure. Now that you are asking me, I'll seriously have to think about it."

Dirk chimed in, "I'm not sure, either. Maybe he should put in a few more Saturdays so we can give you a really accurate assessment."

Keagen was dumbstruck. He thought they might be joking but was terrified they weren't. He was confused and speechless. He really *did* think he had done a good job.

Mr. Jürgen let him hang in suspense for another few seconds, which felt like an eternity to Keagen. Then Jürgen's face lit up with an uncharacteristically huge smile, and his dark eyes sparkled with delight. All three men began to clap their hands and pat him on the back, cheering and whistling.

"You did an outstanding job, Keagen," Jürgen said. "If you were old enough, I would hire you full-time in a second. You have shown a greater work ethic than many adults I've hired." He flashed a grin at his two employees. "You did as we asked, never complained, and worked hard. Truly an excellent job."

Keagen almost collapsed with relief, managing to get out a surprised, "Thanks." When he could think straight again, he asked, "Does this mean you'll speak to Mrs. Stockton?"

"Already have, my boy, already have. She, too, is very pleased with you."

Before Keagen could answer, Jürgen continued, "So, let's sum it up and get you on your way. You worked every Saturday for six weeks, six hours per day. That's a total of thirty-six hours, at a dollar twenty-five per hour, or forty-five dollars."

Keagen was at a loss for words. "Money?" he thought. "Is he talking about money?"

Mr. Jürgen saw his puzzled expression and paused.

"You—are going to pay me?" Keagen asked, not believing his ears.

"Well, of course," Mr. Jürgen replied. "Nobody works for free. Besides, you earned it." He pushed an envelope filled with cash toward Keagen.

Keagen stared at the money, and then at Jürgen, mouth agape. He had not seen this coming at all.

"However," Mr. Jürgen went on, "I have a proposition for you." He reached into a shelf below the worktable and pulled out a roll of papers. Keagen recognized them immediately—his blueprints.

"Mrs. Stockton stopped by the other day and dropped these off," Jürgen said. "I believe they are yours?"

Keagen nodded with excitement. He was so happy to see them again.

Mr. Jürgen held the blueprints for a moment before handing them to Keagen. "I took some time to review these, and they are amazingly well-done. You are quite a good draftsman, Keagen. Your eye for detail is remarkable. You even focused on the correct relative dimensions, and your scale calculations are, for the most part, pretty right on. Mrs. Stockton told me you did these yourself—that you had no help drawing them. Is it true you used different blueprints out of books on shipbuilding to go by in creating your own?"

"Yes, sir," Keagen replied, pride beginning to well up inside him.

"Amazing." Jürgen shook his head. "You have a great gift."

Keagen was embarrassed by his words, but they felt great, especially coming from a master like Mr. Jürgen. He had always thought his specs for *Arondight* were good, but now he had real, unbiased, professional confirmation. He was floating on a cloud.

"I'll tell you what, Keagen," Mr. Jürgen said. "How would you like to build her on a larger scale? I don't think you're ready yet for a full-size, 180-foot racing sloop, but I've done the math, and the material required to create a 1/24 scale model will run you about thirty-five bucks. Of course, my time would be free, and we can use our machines, though we'd have to work on her only after hours and in slow times. If we go over a bit on material costs, I'll cover it, and you can pay me back by working a few more Saturdays here and there in the shop. When we are done, she will reach about seven and a half feet in length and almost six feet in mast height. We will use your blueprints to build her, and I think she will be a beauty. Are you up for it?"

Keagen stood frozen in complete awe, trying to process what had just happened. Finally, he blurted out, "Oh, wow—that would be so great!" He grasped Jürgen's hand and pumped it up and down, and then they both stepped back, like two great businessmen who had just agreed to the deal of a lifetime. Keagen took thirty-five dollars from the envelope, handed the money to Mr. Jürgen, and asked, "When do we start?"

"Soon, but not today," Mr. Jürgen replied. "Time for us all to go home. Drop by the shop one day next week after school, and we'll start laying plans."

As Keagen, Dirk, and Tim trotted to the front door, Jürgen sat gazing thoughtfully out the smudged windows of the workshop, remembering the life lessons he had learned in Mrs. Stockton's class, many years before.

CHAPTER THIRTEEN

It's Not What You Know, But Who You Ask

One late summer evening just before Keagen was to begin high school, Baron came by to see his young friend. He pecked gently on the bedroom window, waited as Keagen raised the sash, then fluttered into the room, settling in his usual place on the footboard of the bed.

"Hello, Keagen," Baron said. "What are you up to this evening?"

"Nothing much," Keagen replied. "Just reading."

"Ah!" Baron was impressed. "Something mandated by your school, I suppose?"

"What?" Keagen said absentmindedly.

"Your book. Is it one that will be helpful in your upcoming studies?"

Keagen gave his friend a puzzled look. "What are you talking about? It's a comic book, not a boring school book. School hasn't started yet."

Baron heaved a sigh. "Keagen, may I make a comment?" He went on without waiting for an answer. "The reason you fail in school is because you want to fail."

"Why do you say that? I don't *want* to fail. Where do you get that idea?" Keagen's defenses were up. "Besides, I'm not failing, I'm just—not doing all that well."

"Even if you don't like what I'm about to tell you, know that I say it because I care a great deal about you and consider you my dear friend," Baron continued. "If I didn't care about you, I would say nothing and let you go on with your destructive attitude and behavior. Remember what I said, long ago—each of us can benefit from constructive criticism, on occasion."

Now Keagen was decidedly uneasy. Baron had given him much advice and counsel before but had never spoken to him quite so directly. He had no reply.

"You are lazy," Baron said. "By that I mean you would rather believe what others might say about you, or worse, what you tell yourself, than get up and do something to change the situation. 'I'm no good.' 'I'm a failure.' You have fallen into such a trap of self-pity that you now actually believe you are good for nothing. It makes no difference if I assert that you are brilliant, creative, and more than capable. It's as if your hands are over your ears, so you can't hear me."

Baron paused for effect, blinked twice, then stared intently into Keagen's eyes. "You think if you try something and fail, if others laugh at your attempts, that this is confirmation you are a 'loser,' as you call it. You decide it's better not to try at all than make a fool of yourself. The result is defeat. You only truly lose if you give up, and that's what I see you doing, Keagen. You not only decide you can't, but that you don't care. This is what brings great sadness to my heart."

Keagen was sitting on the bed with arms wrapped around his drawn-up knees. Baron hopped from the bedstead to perch on Keagen's forearm. "Consider that if you are the cause of others' laughter, the butt of their jokes, it's because you put yourself there. You do nothing to alter your grades or your athletic prowess. If you really want to silence them, show them you respect yourself and that you have it in you to leave them all in the dust—to become better than they are. Prove to *yourself* who you really are and what you can do."

"But how?" Keagen murmured, with his head bowed. "I'm *not* as smart as they are. No matter how hard I try, I'm just not. And I'm not an athlete. I'm not fast, and I'm not strong, and I proved to the world I'm no good at baseball at the tryouts awhile back."

"I challenge your comment about not being smart. You are one of the brightest students in the entire school. But again, that's not for me to say, rather for you to discover for yourself. As for your physical ability, you may not have the strength and speed you desire now, but with an investment, you can achieve it."

"Investment?" Keagen was puzzled. "You mean money?"

"No, Keagen. There are many kinds of investments other than money. In fact, the most valuable of all is the allocation of time. You can spend your time sitting here, night after night, feeling sorry for yourself and reading your silly comic books, wondering why things are the way they are. Or you can choose to invest your time wisely in something that will produce a desirable return. You could, instead, decide to study and learn. Look at it this way: the quality of what you put in determines the value of what you get out. Put your time into comic books – get nothing of value out."

"Hey, I like comic books! I enjoy reading them." Keagen leaped off the bed, tossing Baron into the air. He landed on the back of the desk chair and smoothed his feathers before continuing the lesson.

"I'm sure you do, but spending your time reading comic books will not improve your grades or your physical fitness, no matter how much you wish that were so. You must decide exactly what you want, why you want it, and whether you are willing to do what it takes to get it. Then, invest your time with dedication, passion, and determination, and you will eventually harvest the rewards you seek. One more important thing to keep in mind—you must make certain your investment is for the right reasons. This really is *not* about getting recognition or proving yourself to other people. Stop trying so hard to impress everyone else and start impressing you."

"But how?" Keagen asked again, more frustrated now. "You make it sound so darn easy, but it's not. Trust me, I know."

"Easy? Did I hear you say easy?" Baron fluffed up his feathers all over again. "Keagen, there is no easy way to the top . . . not even for you, as talented as you are. Our proudest achievements come from mastering difficult moments and overcoming the challenges life puts in the way. No one is ever proud of 'easy' accomplishments. I urge you to give up your childish desire to be comfortable and stop blaming others for your despair. Success will never happen for you if you are not willing to take the first step, no matter how good your excuses are. Only you can get yourself out of this rut. Whenever you get knocked down, stand back up and keep pushing onward. That is how winning is done."

He was silent for a few seconds, catching his breath. Then he said quietly, "Keagan, you are still young, but this is a critical time for you to develop your values and belief system. I'll show you the way if you will let me help you. But you must listen without complaint and do as I say. Are you willing to agree to that?"

Keagen rubbed his temples with his fingers and let out a long sigh. Finally, he looked at Baron and said, "Okay. Deal."

"Excellent! First things first. Back to my initial comment. You are lazy, and we are going to change that, in a hurry."

"What?"

"Discipline, my young friend. Rule Number One in bolstering courage and developing confidence is discipline. We will allocate one hour every day to intensive study time."

"An hour? Is that really necessary?" Keagen blurted.

"I wasn't finished," Baron said. "I was about to say that in addition to studying one hour a day, you will run thirty minutes of track every afternoon. But you questioned my suggestion, and I agree with you. Let's begin with one and a half hours of study per day and forty-five minutes of track . . . one more word and you will be up to two hours of study and an hour of track!"

Keagen frowned but said nothing.

"Rule Two is to break out of what is called your 'comfort zone.' If you only do things you know you do well, you will never do much."

"Yeah, you've told me that before."

"Good, then you understand. We will also measure your efforts so that you can see and appreciate your progress. There are many more rules," Baron went on, "but I believe three are enough for us to get started."

"Three?" Keagen said. "You only talked about two."

"Rule Number Three is to use your smarts and be humble. Would you agree that you will never be able to know it all?"

"That's for sure. Nobody can know everything."

"Correct," Baron acknowledged and added, "But you always can ask the right questions. Say, for example, what are the school subjects you struggle with most?"

"Math," Keagen answered quickly. "I hate math with a passion."

"Go on," Baron said. "What else?"

"Hmm, let's see. I'm not so hot in science, either, or geography. That's all boring stuff. And then there's history. That class takes the prize for most boring of all. I don't get why history is so important. It's done with, it's gone, it's in the past. That class is going to kill me."

"Very well," Baron continued. "We shall focus on those four classes—math, science, geography, and history."

"What do you mean by 'focus?'"

"We'll determine who among your classmates is good in each of those subjects. Who do you think is the best student in math?"

"Gina," Keagen replied. "No question about it. She is very smart. She's also great in science."

"And in geography and history?"

"Cassandra," he said, with a dreamy look. "She is just . . . wonderful. Beautiful and so smart."

Baron chuckled to himself at the sparkle in Keagen's eyes. "So. I want you to ask both Gina and Cassandra to help you improve your grades in those subjects."

"No way!" Keagen shouted. "Over my dead body will I ask Cassandra to help me."

"Calm down, my boy," Baron said. "I understand you have feelings for her. We can find others to help you with those subjects."

"I do not have 'feelings' for her," Keagen replied, red-faced.

Baron pushed ahead. "I didn't mean to embarrass you. Who else excels in geography and history?"

"Claire makes A's in everything, and she's always reading history stuff. She actually seems to like all those things that don't matter anymore. And there's this new boy, Boris, who came at the end of last year. He's a smart guy, but I don't know him very well. I think he's probably going to be good in geography."

"Then that settles it," Baron said with finality. "Your school starts next Tuesday, I believe? By next Friday you will have asked Gina, Claire, and Boris to help you with your homework and studies."

Keagen was uncomfortable. "Gina would probably help me, but Claire and Boris? I don't think so."

"Have you ever asked them?"

"No."

"Well, then. What do you have to lose?"

Keagen shifted uneasily and cleared his throat. "I'm not sure that's such a good idea."

"Ah," Baron said. "Embarrassed for others to learn that you need support?"

"I don't know. It's just not cool to ask them to help me."

"Cool?" Baron raised a feathered eyebrow. "Show me on your report card where there are grades for being 'cool.' You think asking for help is admitting weakness and defeat when in fact it's quite the opposite. Requesting assistance from others shows both strength and humility. It also requires wisdom. We can never know everything; you just said so yourself. People who surround themselves with those from whom they can learn gain a tremendous advantage and prove themselves to be as smart as those providing the learning."

"I don't know, Baron," Keagen said. "It's asking a lot."

"You humans!" Baron exploded. "You always think you have to figure things out by yourself. Your ridiculous pride keeps you from reaching out, even when you know there is so much you don't know. Associate with ten very smart people and within a very short period of time you can absorb and benefit from the cumulative learning of their individual lifetimes. But no—you are worried about being 'cool.'"

He calmed down a bit and went on. "To change your life, start by improving your grades. Do what it takes to make that happen. Are you willing to keep the agreement you just made with me?"

"Yes," Keagen whispered, somewhat taken aback by Baron's outburst.

"All right, good. By next Friday you will have asked Gina, Claire, and Boris to assist you."

"But what if they say no?"

"How you ask determines the outcome," Baron said. "If you simply walk up and ask them for help, it's possible they may refuse. You must make your request in such a way that they will say yes."

"Like what?"

"Help them first understand the background for what you are about to ask," Baron explained. "For example, you told me all three are smart and good in school. Have you ever told them that?"

"No. But everyone knows they're the best in class. They know it, too."

"How do you know whether they are aware of what you and others think about them if you've never told them?"

"So . . . I should tell them?" Keagen hesitated.

"Why not? It's worth a try," Baron replied. "Offer a sincere, heartfelt compliment and ask whether they would be so kind as to help you. By the way, this goes for Gina, too. Just because she is your friend doesn't mean you can automatically expect her help. You still need to show her you respect her intelligence and look up to her in that regard. Let her know that you want her help because she is the best at what she knows and does. Compliments feel particularly good between friends because they tend to be more rare."

Keagen nodded, deep in thought.

"So! Time for me to get on with the evening's hunt," Baron said. "Are you excited about our new venture?"

"I wouldn't go that far . . . but I'll give it a go."

"Very good. We start next week." And he hopped onto the windowsill, unfolded his gigantic wings and sailed into the warm night.

Keagen found it was easy to ask Gina for help and did so even before school began. While they were waiting at the Treehouse for Waldo and DiDi to arrive one afternoon, Keagen paid her the compliment and made the request. She gave him a surprised look but quickly agreed to work with him. Asking Claire and Boris, however, was an entirely different matter. It took Keagen several attempts to work up the courage. Finally, he approached Boris between classes.

"Hey, Boris, I want to ask you something," Keagen said, as casually as he could.

"What's up, Keg?"

"Umm, what are you doing next week?" Keagen tried not to sound nervous.

"Not much. Why?" Boris asked, a bit puzzled.

"Well . . . look, you're really good in geography, and I suck," Keagen said. "I was wondering if you could maybe help me out with the homework over the next couple of weeks or so. I mean, if you're cool with that, of course."

"Sure," Boris replied without hesitating. "Tell me when and where."

Keagen was stunned by how easy it was. Claire's reaction was similar, and she added that she was flattered Keagen thought so highly of her. He had tormented himself with worry they would turn him down, and he would be totally embarrassed, but nothing remotely like that had happened. There were no questions, no catty remarks, no judgement. Both were more than willing to help, and Keagen was relieved and rather proud of himself.

The daily running proved more challenging. Keagen started slowly, but week by week he became faster, gaining strength and endurance. Baron was a compassionate but relentless coach, urging Keagen to push himself both physically and academically and never allowing him to quit.

"The moment you stop, the instant you think you've done enough, others will surpass you," Baron reminded him, over and over. "Progress is only possible when you choose to do more than others think is reasonable."

As months passed, the efforts began to pay off. Keagen's grades improved, and he grew slimmer and stronger. He liked the changes he saw in the mirror and started to feel better about himself, taking more care with the way he dressed and wore his hair.

Not only did his look change, but classmates and teachers alike noticed his entire demeanor had shifted. There was an ease and certainty now in how he carried himself. Keagen was building self-confidence.

CHAPTER FOURTEEN

The Trap

Keagen's junior year was well under way when he, Gina, and DiDi gathered again at the Treehouse on a golden, late fall afternoon.

The three were skipping smooth, flat rocks on the lake's surface, competing for who could achieve the most jumps. It had been a long time since they had played this game. Their afternoons, evenings, and weekends were full of activities now, leaving less time for the simple pleasures they had delighted in when they were children. Visits to the Treehouse these days were infrequent, but they still met on occasion to share the events of their lives in an environment that was calm and nurturing.

Had any of the three looked up, they would have noticed two owls sitting side by side on a branch of the tire swing tree, high above their heads. One was a large, brown-and-black-flecked Eagle Owl and the other a much smaller, pure-white Snowy Owl. Both followed the activities of the teenagers with great interest but turned their heads suddenly toward the sound of something approaching rapidly from the small forest path.

Waldo burst through the undergrowth and pushed his bike toward the clearing by the lake where the other bikes lay scattered, dropping his carelessly on top of them. He was in a great hurry and breathing hard, sweat running down his face.

"Keagen, *Keagen*," he shouted as he ran toward his friends.

"What's the matter with you?" Gina demanded.

Completely ignoring her, Waldo went straight to Keagen but was so out of breath no one could understand what he was trying to say.

"Slow down," Keagen tried to calm him. "What's got into you? Are you all right?"

"You are in danger," Waldo finally managed to say.

"Who is?" Gina asked.

"Keagen." Waldo bent over at the waist, still gasping, then collapsed onto his knees.

"Why should I be in danger?" Keagen asked, a slight smile tugging at the corners of his mouth. Waldo could be dramatic at times.

"Franco," was all Waldo could say.

"For crying out loud," Gina snapped. "Calm down and tell us what is going on."

"Franco's mad," Waldo stumbled along. "Sam overheard him talking. He's fuming because you got a better score than he did on the last math test. He says he's gonna hurt you."

"The scores aren't even out yet," DiDi chimed in. "How does Franco know what grade he got if we don't have our tests back?"

"Beats me," said Waldo. "But apparently he knows, and he is not happy. Mr. Heldrich probably told him. You know he favors Franco."

"Why the heck would Franco care what grade I got on a math test?" Keagen mused. "What difference does that make to him?"

"Oh, come on, Keagen—you know Franco's been doing a slow burn about you over the past three years," DiDi retorted. "He thinks you're out to make him look bad whenever you can. And then he asked Cassandra out, and she said no because she already had a date with you."

Keagen reddened. "But . . . I don't have it in for him. I don't have any desire to fight with him, about anything. He's the one who's always picking on me. I'm always the butt of his jokes, though he's not doing that as much anymore."

"Oh, forget about Franco! That's fantastic news about your math test, Keagen," Gina said, giving him a big hug. "I knew you could do it. You worked so hard, and I'm so proud of you."

"Great," Keagen said sarcastically. "I finally get a half-decent score in math, and now I have to die because of it."

Gina looked at him over the top rim of her glasses. "A bit much, don't you think?" she said.

"You don't know how it is to be hated," Keagen defended himself, only half-joking this time.

Gina squared her shoulders. "Franco and his gang have done things to you before. It can't be that bad."

"I'm afraid it is . . . or will be," Waldo moaned, still very distressed.

"Exactly what did Sam tell you?" DiDi asked.

"They're planning an ambush."

"A what?" Gina burst out.

"You know, an ambush, a trap," Waldo repeated, turning back to Keagen. "Tomorrow morning they're going to lay a rope across the steepest part of the hill that leads down to the campus. They know lots of kids will be out in front of the school building, so they'll have an audience. You will be going fastest when you get to the rope. They'll pull it tight from each end and swipe you clean off your bike."

"Those bastards!" Gina jumped to her feet, fuming. "We could tell Principal Alston, but we know he won't do anything. So I'll contact the police and have them arrest Franco and his gang. They are criminals and need to be locked up."

Keagen was silent, sitting cross-legged with his elbows on his knees and hands supporting both cheeks. He stared out at the lake, deep in thought.

"There's not much we can do," DiDi said, trying to calm Gina down. "The police aren't likely to get involved until something has happened. They've got other things to do besides hang around, based on a rumor. And even if it did happen, how could we prove it was Franco's doing?"

"But we need to do something," Gina pressed.

"Waldo," DiDi went on. "How sure are you that you can trust Sam as a source? Is it possible he overheard something and made it a bigger deal than it actually is? Maybe they just want to scare Keagen and told that story because they knew Sam was listening."

"It's possible," Waldo said slowly, "but highly unlikely. Sam told me he heard every word. He was in a stall when Franco and his buddies came into the boys' bathroom. They went over their plan in detail. Sam was so scared he pulled up his feet and didn't even breathe. If they'd known he was in the bathroom, he would probably be in bad shape right now."

DiDi nodded. "Well, there *are* some things that can be done. Keagen can get a ride to school with somebody tomorrow, or walk. Or he could take a different route."

"Or he could take a sick day," Waldo added.

Keagen stood up suddenly and walked to his bike without looking back or responding to any of his friends' remarks.

"Where are you going?" Gina asked.

"Home," he said simply. "I want to be alone for a while." He pushed his bike down the path, calling over his shoulder, "See you tomorrow."

The three sat wordlessly on the sandy ground, watching him depart.

Finally, DiDi spoke. "He's been on the receiving end of the 'Franco Comedy and Torture Show' long enough, don't you think?"

"Their pranks have always been embarrassing but really didn't hurt him physically—well, except for the baseball tryouts," Gina said. "This one is going too far."

"Yep, remember when they taped stinky cheese under his desk?" Waldo said. "The smell was awful, and everybody, including me, thought it came from Keagen. Poor guy went to the bathroom three times to wash his feet. And of course, the class couldn't stop laughing."

"Or when they threw him into the dumpster, and he got covered with spaghetti sauce and leftovers," Gina recalled. "Or when they put his bike on the roof of the school. It took the maintenance crew over two hours to get it back down."

"Okay, enough already!" DiDi said. "Yes, it's been really bad."

"Criminals," Gina said again. "So, what do you think he'll do tomorrow?"

"No idea," Waldo answered. "Stay home, I reckon. I know that's what I would do if I were in his shoes."

"But you heard him," DiDi mused. "He said, 'See you tomorrow.' Guess we'll just have to wait and hope he changes his mind about walking into Franco's trap."

The two owls had remained motionless on their tree branch, listening to the entire conversation. Now they looked at each other, blinking their enormous orange eyes.

Baron whispered, "Are you thinking what I'm thinking?"

LaLa replied with a smirk, "If you're thinking we should help Keagen kick those bullies' butts then yes, I'm thinking what you're thinking."

"Language," Baron said with gentle disapproval.

"Sorry. What's the plan, Dad?"

"I have an idea. Let's pay a visit to Keagen and discuss our strategy." Both spread their wings and glided into the approaching dusk.

The next morning, DiDi, Waldo, and Gina waited nervously in the large, open area next to the school parking lot. The space was shaded by a few big trees and dotted with a handful of benches and picnic tables. Many of the students gathered here each morning, chatting in small groups according to class and social clique, waiting unenthusiastically for the first bell to ring. The trees were set far enough back from the street to allow a clear view of the steep road leading down to the school.

The three friends had already heard the buzz. Franco's associates had been hard at work promoting an "anonymous rumor" that something funny was going to happen out in the road before school today. Attention turned to the steep hill. Suddenly, someone shouted, "Here he comes!"

Keagen came flying down the hill on his bike. "Oh, I can't watch," Gina wailed, covering her eyes, but Waldo and DiDi couldn't look away.

"What is he doing? Why is he here?" DiDi said miserably, under his breath.

As Keagen approached the spot where Franco and his troops had planted the rope, he braked suddenly, wheeled his bike around to a full stop, and waited.

Seconds passed, with the schoolyard crowd's attention still riveted on Keagen. Then heads popped up from the ditches on either side of the road, twenty yards down from where he sat motionless on his bike. Franco's team realized their plan had been foiled, and he and his gang, headed by Spike and Katrun, walked into the road and started menacingly up the hill toward Keagen.

A loud whirring sound stopped them in their tracks. Looking up, they saw a dark cloud crest the top of the hill and move down toward Keagen and Franco's crew. An enormous flock of birds of all types, large and small, swept overhead, circled the group and simultaneously dumped droppings, covering them almost completely with excrement. Keagen was untouched.

Almost as quickly as the birds arrived, they disappeared into the woods flanking the road. The schoolyard erupted in surprised shouts, then laughter and applause.

Keagen walked his bike slowly down to where the boys were slipping and flailing about in the puddles of bird feces, wiping the dripping mess off their heads and faces. He put the kickstand down on his bike, reached into the saddlebag and pulled out a small, clean towel, then walked over to Franco and handed it to him.

"I'm declaring a truce, Franco," Keagen said. "I don't want to be your enemy, and I'm not going to be the butt of your stupid jokes anymore. I'm even willing to be your friend. But this kind of stuff has to stop. I've got friends in this school, and in other places, too." He looked down at the river of bird poop and back at the stone-faced Franco. "Don't mess with me."

Then he mounted the bike and rode down the hill, whistling.

CHAPTER FIFTEEN

———— ✺ ————

Graduation

The months raced by, and almost before Keagen knew it, he was a senior. His last year in high school proved a joyful one, for the most part.

Baron continued to keep him focused on strengthening his study habits and holding to his exercise routine, not to mention providing much coaching around his social skills. His grades improved slowly but steadily, and he found he needed much less tutoring from Boris, Gina, and Claire. To his amazement, he even found himself enjoying some of the classes and homework.

His growing academic prowess was met with satisfaction by Mrs. Stockton and several of the other teachers and by dismay and suspicion on the part of Mr. Heldrich and Miss Nepita. The pair often intimated he was cheating without making any outright accusations, though once Keagen was forced to retake a math test with Mr. Heldrich watching to ensure no foul play. He scored a ninety-five, and Mr. Heldrich had no choice but to give him an A, noting sourly, "Well, I suppose even a blind chicken finds a kernel of corn now and then."

Keagen's physical development was even more noticeable. Baron was ever-vigilant in holding him to his running schedule, and his round, "keg" shape gave way to a lean, strong build.

It seemed to his teachers, friends, and family the changes had happened overnight. Keagen just smiled at comments to this effect, proud of the hard work and willpower that had produced the pleasing result.

While he didn't rank in the top ten in academics, neither was he anywhere near the bottom. He wasn't elected a school favorite, though he now had many friends. In the spring of his senior year, Coach Willard finally relented and added Keagen to the roster for the varsity baseball team, impressed with "how the boy has toughened himself up." Though he mostly warmed the bench, it was a dream come true, and Keagen worked hard, earning the respect of both players and coach.

He grew even closer to Baron's family and the community of owls, though with the exception of Baron, he saw them less often now. They had long since moved back to Owls' Meadow, and Keagen's life had become more full. He found he had less and less time for lovely, lazy afternoons in the glade beside the little stream.

Since the birds had come to Keagen's rescue against Franco and his gang, DiDi, Waldo, and Gina had become more curious than ever about Keagen's connection with the animals in the forest. They were aware he had a "pet" owl but had no idea about his ability to communicate, or of Baron's role in Keagen's transformation. Though they pestered him relentlessly with questions about the bird bombardment, Keagen merely grinned, shrugged his shoulders, and said nothing.

Most surprising was that, to Keagen's immense relief, Franco's bullying did indeed cease. Keagen did not learn the reason, as the two boys never spoke again. He suspected, however, that Franco was intimidated by what must have seemed supernatural powers on Keagen's part. While the other students dismissed the timely appearance of the flock of birds as a lucky coincidence, Franco chose always to give Keagen wide berth, staring at him on occasion with a mixture of fear and resentment.

Keagen was surprised that, on most days when he woke up and thought about the coming school day, he didn't dread it as he once had.

"So, Keagen." Gina smiled at him, looking like the cat that swallowed the canary. It was a chilly Saturday night in April, a month or so before their graduation. The four were huddled under blankets in front of a small fire they had built on the bank of Silver Lake near the Treehouse.

"So, what?" Keagen replied.

"Our days are almost over."

"You make it sound like we are all about to die," DiDi said.

"School days, I meant to say. You're such a smart aleck." She punched DiDi gently in the ribs, and he responded by tickling her.

"Hey, you two," Waldo said, looking at them in mock disgust. "Not in public, please. Save your making out for later. God, you two don't even sound like you when you talk to each other anymore. Gross. I'm going to puke."

Waldo had always thought Gina had a crush on Keagen, but less than a year earlier he, and to a lesser extent, Keagen, were taken by surprise when Gina and DiDi announced they were "going steady." Keagen had known for a while that DiDi harbored feelings for Gina and was glad his friend had finally made a move and asked her to become his girlfriend. Waldo was a little less thrilled, since, with Keagen now dating Cassandra, he was the only one of the gang without someone special in his life.

Having secured parental permission, the four friends stayed at the lake until late into the night. They swung on the tire, shoved each other into the frigid lake and then dried off by the fire, toasting marshmallows on sticks and smushing them onto graham crackers with chocolate to make s'mores. As they laughed and re-told stories about the trials and triumphs of their high school days, they reveled in their close friendship and reflected wistfully, and silently, on Gina's words. This special time in their lives was indeed coming to a close, and soon their circumstances would change in very big ways.

"So, Keagen," Gina said again, carefully turning her marshmallow in the flames. "Is it true? Are you really giving one of the speeches at graduation?"

"Not sure yet," Keagen answered, staring fixedly into the fire.

"That's so great that they asked you!" Waldo exclaimed.

"I guess so. I have to let them know by this Friday."

"Nervous?" Gina teased.

"Well, yes. I mean it's kind of a big thing . . . standing in front of hundreds of people, my dad and all. I'm not sure I can do it. What happens if I forget what I'm trying to say, or mess up?"

"Oh, don't be silly. Of course you can do it," Gina said matter-of-factly.

DiDi clapped him on the back. "Keg, I can't think of anyone I'd rather see on stage closing out our school years than you, and I know most of the rest of our class feels the same way."

"DiDi?" Gina was about to begin her lecture.

"Sorry, so sorry . . . Keagen, I meant to say."

"How did you get asked to do it, anyway?" Waldo wanted to know. "Aren't the speakers always the ones with the best grades?"

"Yes," Keagen replied. "Lauren has the highest grade point average, so she's giving the address as the valedictorian. Boris is the salutatorian, with the second-highest. Usually the class president would speak, too, but James won't be at graduation because he and his family will be in the middle of moving to another city. So, the faculty and Principal Alston decided to ask a student whose grades were 'most improved,' and I'm the one they picked. I have a feeling Mrs. Stockton had a lot to do with it."

"Well, we think you should go for it," Gina said firmly, as the others nodded in agreement.

"I don't know," Keagen said, poking at the embers with a stick. "I just don't know."

Baron weighed in when he paid a visit two evenings later. "You not only can, you must," he insisted, fluffing up his feathers for emphasis. "This is a great honor, and you should treat it as such."

"I'm not so sure," Keagen said.

"Why not?"

"There will be a lot of people," Keagen went on. "Mrs. Stockton thinks there might be as many as five or six hundred, maybe more. We had a big class this year, and everyone will invite their families, friends, and whoever else they know."

"Ah," Baron said. "I see what the problem is. You are frightened."

"I'm not . . . " But before he could finish, Baron interrupted him firmly.

"It's all right to be afraid, Keagen. A strong person is not measured by how little he fears, but rather what he does despite his fear. In fact, that's what defines strength and character. Having courage does not mean you are not afraid. It simply means your commitment to the purpose of your actions outweighs the fear. You can choose to turn this opportunity into one of your greatest moments. Don't shy away from it because you think you might fail. I have taught you better than that over these past few years. If you decline to give this address, you will always wonder how it might have turned out had you chosen to do it."

"Okay, okay, okay," Keagen said, exasperated that he could find no support for backing out. "I get it. You want me to give it a shot. But I don't even know what I'm supposed to talk about."

"Follow your heart, Keagen," Baron said. "Listen carefully, and it will guide you well. Besides, you have been through a great deal in the course of your school years. Look how far you have come, and the stories you could tell. I'm sure writing and delivering this speech will not challenge you nearly as much as you think."

Keagen nodded, still somewhat uncertain.

"How much time do you have to prepare yourself?" Baron asked.

"I have to let Mrs. Stockton know whether I'm going to do it by this Friday," Keagen replied. "Then I've got about a month until graduation."

"Well, don't put it off until the last minute. I'm happy to provide some guidance . . . " Keagen waved off Baron's offer.

"I'll let you know, Baron," he said. "I'm going to think for a while about what I want to say."

The owl made a soft, almost imperceptible clucking sound of tongue against beak and shook his head. "Very well," he said. "I look forward to hearing it."

Baron jumped toward the open window, bid Keagen good night, and disappeared into the dark.

Keagen had a hard time falling asleep that night. He tossed and turned as visions of giving the graduation speech swirled in his head. In one scenario, he stumbled over his words, forgot a large portion of what he had written, and ran humiliated from the stage. This merged into an entirely different version, in which he was a powerful orator, delivering precisely the inspirational message the masses had been waiting to hear—a star on stage, cheered on by millions for his heroic accomplishments.

Before school started the next day, he headed to Mrs. Stockton's classroom to give her the news. The more he thought about it, the more confident he became, and he delivered his answer with a level of hyper-enthusiasm driven by lack of sleep.

"Well, I am glad," she said, satisfied. "I was worried when I asked that you might say no. You seemed a little unsure. Glad to see you've made up your mind. That's wonderful, and I know you will do just fine."

"Oh, I will, and I want to thank you for giving me the opportunity," Keagen sped on.

"No need to thank me, Keagen. You earned the right, and I'm looking forward to your address."

As he headed for the classroom door, she called to him again. "I spoke with Otto Jürgen yesterday afternoon and told him you're graduating in a few weeks. He was wondering if it would be all right for him to come to the ceremony."

"Mr. Jürgen!" Keagen shouted. "Yes, of course. That would be so great. I love that guy!" He was surprised at how emotional he felt that Jürgen was interested in attending his graduation.

"Good," Mrs. Stockton said with an enigmatic smile. "Mr. Jürgen graduated from here many years ago himself. I believe this may be his first visit back since then. You must mean a great deal to him, if he's willing to come back to this building for your graduation. You know, he really struggled in school."

"Mr. Jürgen?" Keagen was baffled. "But . . . he's so smart."

"Oh, yes," Mrs. Stockton agreed. "That he is. But you see, real intelligence isn't measured just in academic scores. There is always more to people than meets the eye, and Otto is a perfect example. In fact, he reminds me of someone else who used to think the world was against him."

Keagen gave her a puzzled look. He was still grappling with the idea that his friend, Mr. Jürgen, the smartest man he had ever met, had had a tough time in school.

"By the way, Keagen," Mrs. Stockton continued, "how is work on the *Arondight* coming along? Have you finished her yet?"

The name instantly cleared his thoughts, and he could barely contain his pride as he answered. "We originally estimated it would take us a couple of years, and it's actually taken longer than that, since

Mr. Jürgen and I only work on her a few hours every other week. But she is really starting to come to life, and she's beautiful. The hull is complete and painted. The inside cabins are all built to spec, and the aft and port decks are almost done. We finished her railings last month, and now we're working on the details of the upper decks— the rudder mechanics and wheel configurations. We will set her masts next month, and then we begin the hard part—laying all the ropes. Can you believe that even though she's just a model, she will still carry more than 300 yards of lines? The last step will be to fit her sails. We estimate we'll have her ready in less than six months. You'll have to see her when we're done. She is magnificent!"

"I can't believe the two of you have stuck with it all this time," Mrs. Stockton said, shaking her head. "I can't wait to see the Wonder of the Seven Seas. Now get on to your first class. I don't want to make you late."

Though Keagen swore to himself he would not procrastinate on writing his speech, he let the time slip by and ended up working furiously to complete it the week before the graduation ceremony.

Baron called on him the evening prior to the event. "So?" he said, as soon as his talons touched down on the sill of the open window. "How is the speech coming along?"

"Great," Keagen said. "It's finished. Do you want to hear it?"

"I would be delighted." Baron settled himself comfortably in his usual spot on the footboard of the bed.

"Okay." Keagen cleared his throat. "Consider yourself honored, because I mentioned you."

Baron fluffed up his feathers and blinked several times.

"Not specifically, of course," Keagen added quickly, "I just sort of . . . made reference to you."

"I see," Baron said. "Now I am even more curious."

"I think it's terrific. I'll just read it as I wrote it, and you can give me your thoughts when I'm done. Okay?"

"Please begin."

Keagan was excited to share his masterpiece with his best friend, and his voice shook a bit as he started.

"I feel honored to be here today to address you fine folks on behalf of my fellow graduates. The past few years have been a roller-coaster ride, full of good and bad and some surprises, but here we are at last, and, I am proud to say, we have prevailed! A friend told me that the most important thing in life is to have a strong sense of self-respect and self-honor. Without that, even the best grades don't mean much. It was good advice, and I've learned to overcome adversity by facing my fear and standing up to people who don't believe in me. To be honest, thinking back, there were many times when I didn't like myself and felt like I was nothing but a big fat failure. I was ready to give up and walk away. But I didn't.

"My friend stood strong and convinced me to stick it out. He taught me to be proud of myself, and that there's nothing you can't achieve if you just believe in yourself. We are capable of so much more than we think we are. We just have to start believing in ourselves. It pays off—trust me on this!

"Another friend told me true intelligence is not always measured in scores and grades. I couldn't agree more. We will be tested out there in the real world, and I sincerely doubt a paper diploma is the only roadmap to a successful life. There is more to it. What exactly? I guess we all have to find that out for ourselves.

"We must choose our own way from here on, and I wish all my fellow graduates the best of luck in finding their path in life. As for me, I have my way mapped out. I plan to accomplish great things in my time, to help others, to foresee and offset adversity whenever I can, and to create strategies to fulfill my dreams, no matter what!

"I know it will require inner strength to master life, but I have learned that opportunities come with possibilities, and I'm willing to

lay it all on the line, to walk up to the edge, and push outward. If we want to achieve greatness, we have to take a chance and fight our fear. We won't be handed things for free, but that's okay—I don't want to get anything for free. I'm willing to work hard for my success, to take nothing for granted, and to show the world that perseverance, dedication, and vision are not just words, but values in the highest code of life.

"I, Keagen Walkabee, Jr., hereby pledge to honor and respect my education by sharing the knowledge I have received and upholding the principles it stands for in my dealings with the rest of the world. I advise my graduating friends to follow suit and create their own life mission according to their own personal concept of winning—a concept that extends far beyond scores on a piece of paper.

"In closing, I would like to recognize a few special guests and friends here in the audience. Mrs. Stockton taught me to never give up, and she fought for me when others did not. Thank you, Mrs. Stockton. I also would like to recognize Mr. Otto Jürgen, who showed me that true success comes not from making good grades, but from attention to detail, concentration on the task at hand, and being the very best at what you do. Thank you, Mr. Jürgen.

"I also would like to thank my parents, my sister, Sallie, and my best friends, Gina, Waldo, and DiDi, for being on my side through some of the most difficult moments of my life. Finally, I want to thank my very best friend, who could not be here in the audience today. I want him to know he is the reason why I've turned out to be pretty indestructible, and why I'm looking at an awesome future. Thank you, my friend—I am grateful from the bottom of my heart.

"Having said all this, I hereby declare our class graduated. Congratulations!"

Keagen looked up from his notes. Baron sat silently, staring at him.

"Well, what do you think?" Keagen asked.

Baron paused for a few seconds more, then said, "Do you want my honest opinion?"

"Of course." Now Keagen was even more nervous.

"Very well, but I want you to remember our conversations about constructive criticism."

"You don't like it," Keagen said, and he could feel tears welling up in his eyes.

"Actually I do like what you have written, were these remarks to be included in your memoirs," Baron said, somewhat gently, "but they are not. You are giving a public address, and what you say should have little to do with you, me, or anything specific that has taken place in your past, unless it is to make a bigger point. You wrote this as a form of self-justification, to prove to them all that you made it, that you came out on top despite how much many of them tried to hold you back.

"Please don't misunderstand me, Keagen. I'm very proud of what you have accomplished over the past several years. It gives me great joy that you have at last found your footing in life, but you are expressing your confidence in a less-than-effective way. Have you ever heard the saying, 'Too little confidence is defeating, but too much is fatal?' Please count the number of times you use the word 'I' in your speech. Your remarks should take the form of uplifting advice to your entire class, not just celebrating yourself."

"I thought that's what I did," Keagen said dejectedly.

"With all due respect, Keagen, your advice comes across as arrogance. You make it sound as if you have it all figured out and no one else does. Please remember that being asked to address your fellow graduates and their guests is an honor, and it is therefore your responsibility to make your audience feel acknowledged, respected, and special. You should speak to them with a confidence that is not self-centered but rather intelligent and visionary. Remember when you told me that one day you would show everyone what you are made of, and that once you did so, everyone would start listening to you?"

"Yes, but that was quite a while back," Keagen said, still feeling he needed to defend what he had written.

"Indeed it was; nevertheless, it bears further discussion now. Your speech is built around that very theme. You overcame your troubled times, and now they had better watch out, or you will use your newfound confidence to get even with some and surpass the rest. How do you think that will leave your audience feeling?"

Baron had moved closer to Keagen now for emphasis, but his tone was still more encouraging than disparaging. "Arrogant people generally have something to hide, and most always, it's their own low sense of self-esteem," he continued. "You are better than that. I hear a sense of self-righteousness in your speech that I think will rub people the wrong way. Most of the people in the audience already know what you have achieved; otherwise you would not have been asked to give the speech in the first place. I suggest you try the opposite approach. A truly confident person does not place himself above others. There is a much more powerful way to communicate your accomplishments—through being humble. People with genuine confidence give others a sense of belonging and make them feel important regardless of rank, title, wealth, or status. To them, everyone is of equal standing, and they communicate this graciously, without making anyone feel out of place."

Keagen listened carefully and at last nodded his head in agreement. "I guess you are right."

"May I give you some guidance by suggesting how I would approach this address?" Baron asked.

"Sure," Keagen said, still deep in thought.

"Wrap your content, your main points, in the form of a story. Don't talk about specifics and what has or hasn't happened. I also suggest you not mention anyone's name, especially those of teachers.

Use a metaphor and make your comments positive and about groups as a whole. People will figure out about whom you are speaking. Talk to them of vision and mission, of goals and principles, of what could be possible! Let their imagination reach far beyond the world of current facts and realities. Take them on a journey and give it an ending that will have them be in awe. They will feel proud and inspired and will never forget the speech you gave at their graduation ceremony.

"I think it would be appropriate to thank your family and your friends, but do not mention me. I know that you treasure our friendship as much as I do. However, you don't have to tell the world in order for me to know how special I am to you. Best friends don't need words. They just know."

This was a lot for Keagen to process, and he sat with his head down, staring blankly at the sheaf of papers in his hands. He didn't know what to think or what actions to take. He was overloaded with the many ideas Baron had presented, and his mind was reeling. Underneath it all was the growing knot in his stomach as he came to terms with the fact that he would have to completely rewrite his speech in less than fifteen hours.

He looked at his dear friend, who was still watching him with great love and concern, and as he focused on Baron, suddenly his fears evaporated.

"May I ask you a personal question?" Keagen said softly. "You don't have to answer it if you don't want to, but I have meant to ask you this for quite a while now."

"Certainly," Baron said. "What's on your mind?"

"I was talking with LaLa some time ago, and she said that you used to be a high-ranking judge, and that you ruled over all the animals in the forest. Is that true?"

"I was indeed a judge for this area, though I did not 'rule,' and I was certainly not in charge of any of the other animals. Why do you ask?"

"LaLa told me you lived in the upper part of the forest in a huge, comfortable treehouse, and that all animals respected and looked up to you. You held the highest rank of honor, she said."

Baron was amused. "Did she, now?"

"Well, what happened?" Keagen said. "You're not a judge any-more, are you?"

"I am still a baron by lineage, but no, I am no longer a judge," Baron said flatly. "I resigned my position, and we moved into a much simpler home."

"You *quit*?" Keagen blurted in surprise.

"I did indeed," Baron replied.

"But . . . why?" Keagen was confused. "It sounds like you were on top of the world. You had all that power—you had *everything*, and you walked away from it?"

"Yes, and I do not regret it for a second. In fact, it was the best decision I ever made." Baron paused thoughtfully. "Power and control are only important to those who have few or no other priorities in their lives.

"You see," he went on, "there are many, even in our world, who offer their friendship and support only to those who are on top. They don't care about the individual, so long as they can latch onto the power that individual has. I never needed or wanted those in my life who didn't really care about me or mine. They were empty souls who certainly did not stand by my side when I hit a rough patch."

"A rough patch?"

"Life is difficult at times, Keagen. No matter how powerful you think you are, no one is more powerful than life itself. You can have everything, and it can all be taken away from you in the flash of a second."

"What . . . do you mean?" Keagen asked hesitantly.

"We lost our baby—unexpectedly. She was beautiful."

Keagen could see the pain in his friend's eyes. "I'm so sorry, Baron. I didn't know."

"No, of course not. I had not told you," Baron said softly. "I think about her often, and though many years have passed, some things never let go of us. Not a day goes by that I don't wish I could have had the chance to give her a wonderful life."

Keagen lowered himself to his knees beside the bed so that he was at eye level with his friend. Wordlessly, he opened his arms and embraced Baron, holding him tightly as tears ran down his cheeks. After a few long moments, Keagen let go, and the two sat in silence for quite some time.

Finally, Baron continued. "There are more important things in life than work, career, rank, title, power, or control," he said. "We certainly have to take necessary steps and make concessions to provide for our families and ensure they flourish. Finding balance is the key. For me, the need to heal my family outweighed my public commitments. My priorities made it an easy choice."

He let out a big sigh. "Promise me you will remember, Keagen, as you get older and start your career, that no matter for whom or where you work, whatever your title may be or whether you run your own company, your family must come first. If you win, so does your family, but if you lose, they will fail with you, too.

"There is simply nothing more important than friendship and family, though many have forgotten that. I may have given up my title, but I did not lose my values or principles. I was no more important when I was a judge than I am today, though many in the animal world don't agree. And, I genuinely do not care what they think."

"Was that when you adopted LaLa? You did adopt her, didn't you?"

"Yes, from a land far away. But please don't think we saved a little owl. I truly believe she was sent to save us. And she has, in every possible way."

Again the friends were silent for a moment.

"Now let me ask you a question, Keagen," Baron said. "Are you telling me that you would respect me more if I were still a judge?"

"Of course not!" Keagen exclaimed. "I love you for who you are. I don't care what you did or what you do."

"I thought as much, Keagen. Yes, I did," Baron said, with great satisfaction. "You are one of the good ones; you have a pure heart. Stay true to your gift. Don't get blindsided by society or let others tell you what you are not and who you should be. Besides, if I were still a judge, I would not have any time to 'hang out' with this crazy human being I met a few years ago."

Both started to chuckle.

"So you think I should rewrite the speech?" Keagen posed it as a question, though he knew the answer. "You think I can do better?"

"What I think is not important, Keagen," Baron said. "And it is not a matter of making your speech better or worse. It's about what's in your heart and what you are really trying to convey.

I know you have a story to tell, and I believe you can do so without assigning blame or using the things that have happened in your past as a scoreboard against the present. Leave your past where it is.

"You and I know how hard you have worked to get where you are today. It's a fact you can be proud of, and which can be your silent triumph as you go onto the stage and deliver your address with humble confidence. Give them a speech so powerful that no one in the audience, neither your peers, nor teachers, nor parents and guests will ever forget. Share your message in such a way that each of them will take it out into the world as their own."

Now Keagen was overwhelmed again, and he looked at Baron in panic. "Can you help me with it?"

"Oh no, my friend," Baron replied. "You don't need my help. I promised you guidance, and that is exactly what I have provided. I have watched you grow up over the years and given you some pointers along the way, but this is your time."

Baron straightened up and shook out his feathers, a sign that he was about to leave. He hopped onto the sill of the open window but turned back once again. "You can't fail, Keagen. No matter what happens tomorrow, I want you to know I'm very proud of you and consider myself blessed to have you as my friend." Before Keagen could respond, Baron leaped into the darkness and was gone.

Keagan picked up the speech, crumpled the pages into a ball and hit a perfect three-pointer into the trashcan across the room by his desk. "Winner!" he shouted. Then he took out a blank piece of paper, grabbed a pen and tried to clear his thoughts. He knew the next several hours would be some of the longest in his life.

CHAPTER SIXTEEN

The Speech

Keagen looked up and down the boisterous line of his fellow graduating seniors, waiting in a hallway to march into the school auditorium. Most, he figured, would have a few butterflies in their stomachs. They would be a little nervous about stepping onto the stage to receive their diplomas.

But if they had butterflies, Keagen felt as if he had eighteen-wheelers roaming around inside him. He had never been so nervous in his life. He closed his eyes and tried to block out the noise and ignore the cold sweat running down his spine. His kneecaps began to shake, and his heart was beating like a jackhammer. He was sure he was going to be sick.

As he steeled himself for a run to the restroom, he felt someone grip his shoulder. He opened his eyes and saw Otto Jürgen standing in front of him with a big grin on his face. Jürgen's expression changed to concern when he saw how pale Keagen was.

"Are you all right, son?" Jürgen said in a low voice.

"Not really," Keagen mumbled.

"A little anxious about your address?"

"I . . . I guess so."

"You will be great. No worries. I will cheer for you!" Jürgen gave him an encouraging pat on the shoulder and walked toward the auditorium. Keagen bolted for the boys' restroom, where he did not, could not, throw up. He leaned against the cold tile wall, fanning himself with the pages of his speech, then splashed water on his face at one of the basins, trying not to get his graduation robe wet.

Now he could hear the muffled sounds of the school band playing "Pomp and Circumstance," and he hurried back to his place in the line, which had begun to move. The soon-to-be graduates started filing into the second row of seats. The front row was reserved for faculty and a handful of VIP guests. Seated on the stage were Principal Alston, the assistant principal, and the featured graduation speaker, a successful local businessman.

Keagen looked nervously over his shoulder at the crowd. The auditorium was packed. There were nearly a thousand people, he estimated, more than twice what he had been told to expect.

He started to feel queasy again until Gina, who by alphabetical last name was seated next to him, reached over and squeezed his hand. He immediately felt better and looked around once again, spotting his parents, who were all smiles. His father caught his eye and gave two thumbs up. Sallie, who was now a junior in college, sat next to them. She looked completely bored, as usual, and that made Keagen laugh, releasing some of his tension. "Thanks, Sallie," he thought.

He actually liked her more than he let on. She was cool on the outside but deep and thoughtful on the inside, though she certainly wouldn't want that to be known. He admired her courage and her strength. Sallie went her own way, swimming upstream regardless of the consequences, and that made her popular. Keagen wished he were more like her.

When the graduating class was seated, Principal Alston stepped to the podium and began speaking, though Keagen's mind was racing so fast he couldn't grasp what was being said. He tried to focus his attention on something else, and peered through the sea of graduation caps before him at the teachers on the front row. There was

Mrs. Stockton, which made Keagen smile. He spotted Mr. Heldrich and Coach Willard, both looking, it seemed to Keagen, as if they were personally responsible for the fact that these students had made it to the finish line. "Typical," he thought. "Just like pufferfish—pretending to be more than is actually there."

Principal Alston introduced the featured speaker, who launched into his remarks. Keagen leaned his head back and closed his eyes. Something had him open them again, and he saw, perched in one of the skylights in the ceiling of the old auditorium, far above the crowd, three familiar figures—Baron, Salamona, and LaLa. They had come to give him moral support. Keagen grinned and gave a little wave. He realized his nausea was almost gone, though his hands were still shaking.

Next on the program was the speech by the salutatorian, followed by the valedictory address. Then the principal and assistant principal began calling the graduating students to the stage, one by one, to receive their diplomas.

The long black graduation robes and matching caps were edged in beige, reflecting the school colors, and gave the ceremony a sense of elegance and importance. The seniors stood one row at a time and queued up at the steps leading to the stage to await their names being called.

Keagen's thoughts were still wandering when he felt an elbow to the ribs on his right side. It was Gina, urgently motioning him to move. His head whipped to the left. The seats on his row were empty, and he heard Principal Alston calling out, apparently for the second time, "Keagen Walkabee."

He jumped to his feet and raced down the aisle. Scrambling up the steps, his foot caught in the hem of his robe, and he almost landed face-first on the stage, regaining his balance in the nick of time. Laughter and a smattering of applause rippled through the audience, and Principal Alston rolled his eyes as he handed Keagen his diploma and shook his hand.

When the presentation of diplomas was complete and the newly minted graduates were back in their seats, Principal Alston approached the podium once more. "We have one final speaker today," he said. "This young man surprised us all by challenging our initial perceptions. Keagen started off as an average student, and many of us thought he would end up the same way. But over the past two years, he has really turned things around—so much so that he is graduating as one of the school's honor students. Well done, Keagen, well done."

The audience applauded politely, and the principal continued. "He didn't get the best scores on his placement exams, but they were respectable enough that he stood out. His impressive improvement led the faculty to invite him to be our final commencement speaker. Ladies and gentlemen, Keagen Walkabee."

Keagen took a deep breath and reached inside his robe for the speech he had tucked into his shirt. His blood ran cold. It—wasn't—there. Impossible! What, where? He flashed back on the events of the morning and immediately remembered. He had left it beside the sink in the restroom.

He thought for a moment he would pass out but willed himself to stand, still clutching his diploma, and walk back down the aisle, up the steps and across the stage to the podium, which he grasped as if it were a life preserver.

He looked out over the crowd and swallowed hard. Then he cast his eyes up once again to the distant rafters, where he could see Baron fluffing his feathers. Keagen chuckled softly and began:

"Principal Alston, members of the faculty, my fellow graduates, family, and friends—it is with great honor that I stand here before you today. I feel privileged to have been given the opportunity to address

you. We seniors have just completed a major milestone in our lives and are approaching a future that has yet to be written. If I have learned anything over the past twelve years of school, it is that we have the ability, and the responsibility, to write our own future, through the choices we make, the paths we take, and the values we apply.

"That might sound pretty clear and simple, but I have to tell you, my parents scared the living bejesus out of me when they said that I'm all grown up now and have to act responsibly! I know I'm not ready for that, whatever it means!"

Soft laughter fluttered through the audience.

"Before I actually begin my speech, I would like to thank a few individuals who have taught me so much and stood by my side through some turbulent times along the journey that's brought us all to today.

"First, my best friends, Waldo, Gina, and DiDi, who showed me that friendship is not just a word, but the sum of many things. It's about acceptance without judgment, unshakable trust, and unfailing loyalty. I cherish my friendship with them and will for the rest of my life. Thank you, guys."

This elicited mild applause.

"Then there are my parents, who have tried hard to make something out of me. For the past dozen years, they have told me every day to do my homework! I thought they would get tired of repeating the same thing over and over, but no such luck. I'm not sure whether they've managed to actually make something out of me, but I would at least give them the award for trying. Thanks, Mom and Dad. I love you.

"Oh yes—I can't leave out my big sis. Some of you remember her—she graduated from here three years ago. Thanks for putting up with me, Sallie. I know you miss all the mutual torment now that you're away at college."

The audience laughed, and Sallie gave him a displeased look, then stuck out her tongue.

"I also would like to thank Mr. Otto Jürgen, who taught me that dedication, hard work, and precision can create things of greatness and beauty. Of course, I want to recognize my teachers for their efforts and for showing me—all of us—the ropes. Thank you."

Keagen said this while looking directly at Mrs. Stockton, who smiled broadly as the audience applauded again.

"My greatest thanks go out to a dear friend who's had more to do with my 'turnaround,' as Principal Alston called it, than anyone. He asked me not to mention him in this speech, but it wouldn't be right to leave him out. From the bottom of my heart, thank you for helping me end my period of invisibility and realize that I'm worth more than I ever thought I was. You have given me the confidence to discover myself and to live my life with passion and courage and heart. I owe you everything. I love you and am eternally grateful."

The audience buzzed with confusion at Keagen's nameless reference, but he had found his rhythm now and continued undeterred.

"I spent a lot of time writing a speech I thought would be appropriate for this occasion. I threw it away last night and wrote a new one, which I accidentally left in the restroom earlier today. Sometimes we just have to deal with the unexpected and make the best of things we didn't see coming. Most of my new speech was a story. Let's see if I can remember it all.

"Way back, almost a century ago, people traveled across America in stagecoaches. They were the buses of the Wild West. A team of horses pulled the coach and brought people from Point A to Point B. Back then, you could buy three types of tickets to travel.

"The first-class ticket, as you probably figured, was the most expensive. So it was usually bought by people of rank, those who had wealth and status. With a first-class ticket you traveled in comfort inside the coach, seated on plush cushions, and you were provided with refreshments along the way. If the stagecoach got stuck in a mudhole, or the road was blocked by a fallen tree or boulder, or they came upon

a really steep hill, the people with a first-class ticket remained comfortably seated in the coach until the problem was resolved and the journey continued.

"Then there was the second-class ticket—much less expensive, but also a less-comfortable ride. No cushions, no refreshments, just a seat and a way to get where you needed to go. When the stagecoach got stuck, the folks with a second-class ticket had to get off the coach, rain or shine, and wait by the roadside or walk alongside until the problem got fixed and the trip went on.

"Finally there was the third-class ticket. This type was purchased by people with little money, oftentimes laborers who needed to hitch a ride from town to town across the frontier to find work. The third-class ticket did not secure a seat at all. Ticketholders might sit on top, or stand on the back, clinging to the luggage, or ride holding onto the sides of the coach. Whenever there was a mudhole or a roadblock or a steep hill, the third-class passengers were expected to get off and help overcome the obstacle or push the coach."

Keagen paused and held up his diploma triumphantly. *"Every one of us today received a first-class ticket to life. We worked hard for it, we earned it, we deserve it!"*

The students exploded into wild applause and shouts. The noise was deafening for a few seconds, and Keagen waited for it to die down before going on.

"The advice I have for my fellow graduates is . . . don't use that first-class ticket. Instead, whenever we run into a mudhole or roadblock or steep hill in our lives, let us choose not to remain comfortably seated on the coach while others push us out of the situation.

"Instead, let's get off our 'stagecoach' and help push. One hundred years from now, it won't matter how big a house we lived in, or what kind of car we drove, or what title we held in the company we worked for. But we may be remembered for being kind and providing support to a little child, or lending a hand to someone who desperately needed

it, or offering forgiveness. These are the kinds of things that can change lives, and those whose lives are changed may then reach out and change others.

"To me, this diploma is not just a piece of paper with names and dates marking the end of something. It's a declaration of a beginning, the beginning of the rest of our lives. I urge my colleagues to seek a purpose in life that extends well beyond getting a good job and making a living. A great man said, 'We might make a living by what we get, but we make a life by what we give.'

"May our diplomas be a constant reminder of what's possible when we make the commitment to be different, to live differently, and to make a difference.

"Ladies and Gentlemen, congratulations to all of us! I hereby declare our class graduated!"

There was an instant of utter silence as Keagen stood at the podium, eyes closed and out of breath, holding up his diploma once again. Then the entire auditorium was on its feet, cheering, clapping, and waving their arms. The graduating seniors threw their caps high into the air. Principal Alston walked forward and shook Keagen's hand, and then, as if he were in a dream, Keagen moved slowly across the stage and down the steps into the mass of graduates. He was surrounded by well-wishers, hugging him, complimenting his address, and celebrating his words of wisdom.

Through the din of the crowd, he heard a soft voice whisper in his ear, "Not only was this the most amazing thing I have ever heard, it was spoken by the man I love. Keagen Walkabee, Jr., you are incredible."

Keagen turned and found himself looking into the eyes of the most beautiful person in the world—Cassandra, the woman of his dreams, who had done him the honor of agreeing to go steady just the weekend before. She gave him a quick but passionate kiss on the lips, right there in front of the whole audience, and they walked out of the auditorium hand-in-hand.

"So, my hero," Cassandra said, as they strolled down the sidewalk in front of the school. "What's next for you?"

"I'm not sure," Keagen said. "A good friend suggested I think about a career in design, or architecture, or business. But he also thought it would be a good idea for me to spend some time in the service industry first."

"Does this friend have a name?"

Keagen stopped walking and turned to her with a quizzical look. She smiled. "And does he have feathers?"

"Cassandra, I—you—um . . ." Keagen was at a loss, and his face was scarlet.

She laughed and clasped both his hands in hers. "You don't have to explain. Whoever you've been getting advice from seems to be doing a pretty good job so far. I think you should listen to him." Keagen enveloped her in an enormous, relieved hug.

The commencement celebration continued that evening. Keagen's father had promised him a graduation party, and most of the class attended, along with Mrs. Stockton, Mr. Jürgen, Bert, Cassandra and her parents, Waldo, Gina, DiDi, and a number of other family friends.

As the last guests were leaving, Keagen glanced up into the huge oak tree in his front yard, and saw three pairs of glowing orange eyes. He smiled and could have sworn he saw them smiling back.

"Thank you, for everything," he said. "I love you guys." The eyes blinked simultaneously, then in a whisper of wind and wings, they were gone.

Standoff *in the Glass Tower*

Saturday, 11:32 a.m.

Dalton had reached a stopping point in the story. He looked around at his small audience and noted with satisfaction that they all seemed completely engaged, if still skeptical. Smiling, he said, "Well, my friends, what do you see? What do you hear in what I have shared that might have implications for you at Hoppe Enterprises?"

"Is that the end of the story?" asked Karen Singer, the vice president of communications.

"Oh, no, Ms. Singer. There is much more. But we'll pause here to take stock. Thoughts?"

"Well, Keagen certainly learned to stand up for himself, thanks to Baron the owl," she said thoughtfully, as Karl Ruttner rolled his eyes and put his head on the table. "Earlier today you accused us of not standing up to Mr. Ulrich. Exactly how do you suggest we do that?"

"You are asking the wrong question, Ms. Singer," Dalton countered.

"What should I ask, then?"

"A much more useful inquiry might be, 'How can I stay true to my values and principles regardless of the boss I have?'"

"Clearly you don't know Mr. Ulrich very well," chimed in Michelle Beckwith, the human resources head.

"That's true," Dalton replied. "But do I need to know him in order to understand *your* behavior?"

"What do you mean, *our* behavior?" said George Bennett, the vice president of customer care. "If we're being completely frank here, Ulrich is a terrible CEO and an even worse human being. It's not our fault the company is going down the tubes."

"Ah, I see. Identify the source of your miserable circumstances and blame it. That way, the outcome is irrelevant, because you have a tidy excuse to offer up instead of taking action yourselves."

Tom Murray, the vice president of global sales, slapped both hands down on the conference table. "Why do you keep trying to lay this whole thing at our feet? Why are you in denial that Ulrich is the problem?"

"Is he, Mr. Murray?"

No one else spoke. The entire group was fixated on Dalton.

"I want you all to listen to me carefully," he said, his voice quiet but intense. "There will always be people out there in your world who are not living up to your standards—people who are rude, mean, inconsiderate, cold, ruthless, or just plain stupid. That will never change.

"Today it's your CEO. Tomorrow it will be someone else. You cannot fight them, because you wouldn't stand a chance of winning, and most certainly, you cannot change them. Yet it seems to me they have the power to change you. Take your current situation. Not only has your behavior altered here at work, but I imagine you are very different at home now, too. You bring your frustration and anger about the workplace into your house, and your families end up paying the price for how your CEO runs the company. Is that really how you want your life to go? You are all waiting for Ulrich to suddenly and miraculously be different, or for someone or something else to rectify things, and that could be a long time coming."

Now Dalton stood and began strolling behind the row of chairs on the window side of the table. All eyes followed his moves.

"I believe that you, the company's leadership, are making some fundamental mistakes," he continued. "The first lies in the very core of your thinking. Your attitude is the essence of what's in your heart, but it all starts with the way you think. Thoughts dictate feelings. Feelings generate emotions, and those translate into your actions, or behaviors.

"How you behave shapes 'reality' about you in the eyes of others. If you think defeating thoughts, you feel defeated, and you speak and act in a defeated way. People begin to label you as 'defeated.' Conversely, if you focus your thoughts on things that are positive, you feel better, and your actions follow suit. People think of you as optimistic and upbeat.

"If someone tells you you're not good enough, and you believe it, your behavior will demonstrate this. All the people around you will sense your lack of self-confidence, and as we know, that's the kiss of death in business. But it doesn't stop there. That disempowering core thought will impact your personal relationships with family and friends and just about everything you do. If you don't believe in yourself, why should others believe in you? So naturally, the first step you want to take is to consciously shift your core thoughts. You will be surprised at what happens when you choose to do this."

"So we just snap our fingers, and suddenly we'll be different?" Karl Ruttner asked sourly. "Exactly how are we supposed to not let people like Ulrich affect us? He thinks we are all good-for-nothing idiots. How do we convince him otherwise?"

"There is your next mistake, Mr. Ruttner," Dalton went on, addressing the whole group. "You are trying to impress the wrong person. Do you really think you are stupid? Do your family and friends think you are good for nothing?"

"Well, of course not," Ruttner shot back.

"Then why do you give one person's opinion so much weight? Has it occurred to you that Mr. Ulrich builds his own confidence by diminishing others? His behavior really has very little to do with anyone here in this room. There are many like him, individuals who control their environments by infusing those around them with fear and insecurity. However, this only works when you allow them to do it. There is a better plan: don't fight them."

"Now you've lost me," said Patrick Sahne, vice president of production. "Did I hear this correctly? You just said that we should *not* fight him."

Dalton's eyes twinkled. "Let me explain. Imagine you are a huge oak tree with deep roots. You stand up straight and tall and feel strong and powerful. Whenever a storm approaches, you face the winds head on, because you believe you are invincible, that nothing can destroy you. You win most of those battles, but one day you face a storm stronger than you, with winds able to snap you like a toothpick.

"I think you are all facing such a storm now, and you believe you must be strong and take it head on. But I suggest you stop being such a tough and unbending oak and become more like bamboo. A stand of bamboo is flexible; it sways in the wind and can survive the fiercest of storms that completely destroy sturdier trees. Ultimately, the future does not belong to the strongest, most powerful leaders, but rather to those who master being flexible without breaking."

Susan Richards, the accounting chief, looked confused. "So we should just give in and agree with everything Ulrich tells us to do, and by that show flexibility?" she asked.

"That is not what I said and definitely not what I meant," Dalton replied calmly. "It's healthy to confront your fear and to stand up for what you think and believe. But keep your assertions factual, back up your opinions with data, and most importantly, don't take Ulrich's reactions or anything he says personally. He can only hurt you if you let him."

He let that sink in, then said, "Don't be afraid when you speak with him. Be relaxed but confident and don't argue. The louder he may get, the calmer you become. If he threatens you with consequences, cut the conversation short and depart on a positive note. Through your behavior, let him know that while he may be your CEO, he does not own you. Take a lesson from Keagen. He stood up to his father, despite all his fear, and gained the respect he had been seeking for so many years. He had a similar experience with Coach Willard.

"And, instead of continuing to hide from Franco and his gang of bullies, or retaliate in kind, Keagen stood up to them as well, and extended a hand in peace, which put an end to the conflict. When you are on the side of right, being true to yourself, you cannot go wrong, even if in the moment it seems everything is against you."

There was silence for a few moments, then George Bennett said, almost under his breath, "I wish we had our old CEO back. Things were so much easier then."

"And so much more fun," Karen Singer added.

"I can understand your feeling that way, which brings me to the next unsettling reality," Dalton said. "It seems most of you live either in the past or in the future, and neither is a satisfying or productive place to dwell. You're not alone. Many individuals feel their past was better than their present, and there are even more who survive the realities of the present by hoping, somewhat desperately, but not really believing, that their tomorrow will be better than today.

"Then there are the ones who don't live in the moment because they feel imprisoned by a past so difficult and unfair they've stopped trying to overcome it. These people have lost all hope that life can be any other way.

"And without hope, without that belief, they have no access to confidence, which is what this whole matter is about. Here is my advice to you: your past is gone—leave it there. Your future will come—there is nothing you can do about it. Rather, put everything that matters—your passion, your beliefs and values, your feelings for what and whom you care most—into *this* moment. Right now is what counts, because it is the only point in time over which you actually have any control.

"But truly living in the moment will require you to let go of anger and any disappointments others may have caused you. As human beings, we all have these things in our lives. Think about it—everyone in this room is still angry with someone, or perhaps several people, who have done you wrong in the past. Maybe they cheated you, or failed to keep a promise, or let you down, hurt you, or even tried to do you harm on purpose. You wake up every morning still holding onto those wrongdoings.

"It's as if you have an invisible backpack on your shoulders filled with stuff that happened sometime in the past, yet it continues to wear you down and wear you out. How in the world do you believe you might be able to live better tomorrow than today if you can't let go of what happened yesterday, or years ago? I strongly suggest you take off the backpack of the past. You will actually feel the weight disappear from your shoulders and experience a sense of relief and freedom you didn't think possible."

"You believe what's got us into the mess we're in is *our* crisis of confidence?" said Patrick Sahne. "Not the economy, not competition, not unbelievable mismanagement on the part of Ulrich and his cronies?"

"Not exclusively but yes, confidence has a lot to do with it. The foundation of great leadership is confidence, and confidence can only stand strong if it is aligned with a higher purpose. I assert you have all lost your sense of purpose and so are unable to lead a company, let alone your families or yourselves."

Dalton looked into every face around the table. "Being a vice president, director, or department head is far more than a position description, ladies and gentlemen. Status means absolutely nothing when it's been given to you by a company and presented in the form of a business card.

"If you think you are successful just because you have a title, what will happen when you lose your status? Will you collapse like a house of cards?

"No, when you hold a leadership position, it's your job to create a culture within your part of the organization that's fueled by strength and humility, good decision-making, innovation, risk-taking, creative thinking, and shared values. Most importantly you need to show courage to stand up for what's right.

"*You* are responsible for the growth of this company and its people, as much as Mr. Ulrich. What's more, you are also in charge of shaping the culture within the other parts of your life—with your family, friends, neighborhood, community.

"You complain Mr. Ulrich doesn't listen to you, respect your ideas, or appreciate your contributions. But how much time have you spent lately with the people in your life who truly matter, like your children? Not five or ten minutes at dinner or bedtime, but real 'quality time,' talking, listening, having fun, and laughing, just because you chose to do so?"

No one said a word.

"You needn't answer my question. I know the answer already: not enough, and probably not in a very long time. In my opinion, you are only able to share what you have. So how on earth will you be able to teach your staff and your family what confidence is all about if you have none yourself? In reality, you are not scared of Mr.

Ulrich. You are afraid of yourselves and what might happen if you fail."

Karl Ruttner sat back in his chair and made a face. "Well, none of us has a talking owl in the backyard who can spread his wings and magically instill confidence in us."

Dalton grinned. "Perhaps not. But you are not just twelve years old. And you do have the benefit of having heard this story." He resumed his measured pacing around the conference room.

"Confidence is a function of self-respect and having a purpose in life. It can't be borrowed, bought, or demanded. It's not something we are entitled to, nor is it contingent on anyone else's affirmation or approval. Just because you don't get validation from the person who seems to be in charge doesn't mean you should stop believing in yourself. You don't build self-confidence by doing things you already know how to do well, but rather by trying something new, even though you might fail.

"Building confidence has everything to do with who you are as an individual. Do you stand in front of the mirror and see someone who is powerful, attractive, accomplished, and out to make a difference in your world? Or do you beat yourself up because you think you are not good enough—not handsome or beautiful enough, not smart or bold enough? When will you learn that you are most beautiful on the inside?

"The change you all would like to see in this organization can begin right here, my friends. If you want to save this enterprise—if that is your shared purpose—don't start with the company, start with yourselves. It's time to get back what you've lost, so you can discover again who you truly are—a group of smart, powerful, talented people who are capable of doing just about anything you set your minds to.

"Look to the people who truly matter in your life to tell you who you are. Enrich your life with interests that give you joy, outside the four glass walls of this building. Spend time with your family and friends. Help others in need. This is how you find your center, your sense of self. Then when things go wrong in life, you have a solid foundation in place from which to buffer the tough moments. You have balance, and balance cultivates confidence."

"You make it sound so simple, Mr. Dalton. But our reality looks quite a bit different," said Patrick Sahne. "Our workloads here keep us so busy we don't have time for anything else. Look at us right now. It's Saturday, and we were summoned to spend it here on behalf of someone who is probably out enjoying himself on his yacht right now."

"So you are telling me that your reality would change drastically if Mr. Ulrich were to leave and someone else take over?" Dalton queried.

"Most likely!" Susan Richards piped up.

Dalton had paused to look out the massive windows again. Now he turned back to them. "Would it?" he asked. "I disagree. I believe that, even if the company hired a new CEO, your behavior would change little because of the mental habits you've created—blaming and criticizing others, focusing on the negative, cynicism about what might be possible. Remember the story about the turtle and the scorpion. It was in the scorpion's nature to sting the turtle. Similarly, you have created your 'nature': think and act negatively.

"Here is another example: when your child brings home a report card, and it has six A's and one F, which grade do you zero in on?"

"The F," George Bennett said honestly.

"Exactly," Dalton said. "Even if the company hired a new CEO who was extraordinary, you would still zoom in on his or her faults. It has become your way of thinking. You have created a habit of negativity, and it's likely spilling over into the rest of your life. The good news is that you can change your thoughts and so create new habits.

"Life often hands us unexpected and difficult situations. There will always be bullies in some form to contend with. But I know there is more to each and every one of you than to believe one person has the power to completely destroy your confidence.

"Confidence begins with self-respect. Before you can ask others to respect you, you must start to respect yourselves again. Listen to your own instincts regardless of what others tell you. Stand back up and move forward. Let go of the baggage from the past and realize that letting go is not the same as giving up. Focus consciously on shifting the very core of how you think, and then watch how the way you feel and act will change. Confidence is the father of success, and you only get to truly experience it when you walk to the edge . . . and push outward!"

Dalton paused for a glass of water, then resumed. "It's just like the story of the jumping frogs." The group shot him collective puzzled looks, and he chuckled. "Three frogs were sitting at the bottom of a big hill—a hill so steep no frog in history had ever climbed it. Not that they didn't want to, but it was common knowledge among frogs that this hill could not be climbed and was dangerous besides.

"Despite this, the largest of the three frogs decided to attempt the difficult passage, and many other frogs came out to watch. As he began the climb, the onlookers screamed warnings and urged him to stop. To no one's surprise, the frog lost his footing and rolled all the way back down the hill before he had even reached the halfway point.

"The second frog, who was somewhat smaller, hopped toward the hill and began his climb. More and more frogs from the nearby pond joined the crowd, which was crying out that the effort was crazy and he should give up before he got hurt. As the second frog approached the steepest part of the hill, he, too, slipped and rolled back down.

"Now the smallest frog began hopping up the hill. He kept going and going and going, despite the chorus of calls from the crowd warning him of the danger and begging him to cease the attempt. At one point, one of the frog elders leaped off his lily pad and wandered over to see what the commotion was about. The group pointed to the small frog, who was now at the steepest part of the hill, clamoring that he was in great danger, but they could not get him to stop.

"The elder frog shook his head, saying, 'You can stop shouting—he can't hear you. That's Earless Jumper. He is deaf.' And Earless Jumper made it all the way to the top."

The room was silent, each person lost in thought.

Finally Patrick Sahne spoke again. "So, Mr. Dalton . . . how much of your story is true? Did Keagen Walkabee really keep pet owls?"

"Mr. Sahne, all of my story is true."

"Oh, c'mon!" Sahne laughed. "You're telling us the founder of Hoppe Enterprises could talk to owls? And they talked back? That's just a little bit crazy!"

"Why is it so hard to believe?" Dalton asked.

"Because it's impossible, of course. We're grown-ups here."

"Impossible in your mind, perhaps," Dalton said. "Maybe you have locked up your imagination so tightly, hidden it away so completely, you've lost sight of the amazing things it's capable of conceiving and creating. Your imagination lives much closer to reality than you might think, and it can have a powerful impact on our lives."

He walked closer to Sahne's chair and leaned down. "Mr. Sahne," he said quietly. "You of all people should appreciate the power of imagination. As a child, did you not dream that you could fly? Even in your sleep you could feel the liftoff in your stomach when you flapped your arms."

"How did you . . . " Sahne began, but Dalton pushed on.

"Have you forgotten that dream? And how can you be so sure it was only a dream? We all have dreams we have forgotten. What happened to us? We began to fill our minds with judgement-driven, concrete words like *impossible, never, always, unrealistic.* And our thoughts became our reality. If we live our lives bounded by impossibilities, we will get exactly that, and nothing more. No imagination, no dreams. No dreams, no vision. No vision, no purpose. No purpose, no target. No target, no action. No action, no achievement. No achievement, no confidence!

"The greater your imagination, the greater your dreams, and great dreams give rise to the most effective motivator of all . . . believing. That is what prompts us to action." Dalton paused, pursing his lips and closing his eyes for a second. "You may think what's missing is hope, but hope is just a desperate wish for things to get better. As I look around this table and listen to you speak, it seems to me you need much more than that. I think you need to believe again."

Joe Walt spoke at last. "If I understand you correctly, Mr. Dalton, you are suggesting we need to become more optimistic?"

"Optimism is a good start, Mr. Walt," Dalton said. "But optimism is not the same thing as believing in what's possible. Optimistic people generally have a good bit of self-confidence—maybe not always fueled by well-founded motivation, but confidence nonetheless. They remind me of a quote from the legendary inspirational speaker Zig Ziglar: 'I'm so optimistic I'd go after Moby Dick in a row boat and take the tartar sauce with me.'"

The group broke out in laughter.

"However, I don't think optimism is the remedy for your situation and what you have to overcome," Dalton went on. "I think you need something stronger."

"Go on," said Walt. "We are all ears."

"Consider this," Dalton began again. "Many years ago, seven coalminers got trapped in a deep shaft. The flame from an oil lamp ignited a pocket of methane gas, causing an explosion that collapsed several tunnels including the one where the seven men were working, blocking their way out.

"Some experienced minor injuries from the falling rocks, but overall the group escaped the disaster unharmed. After the shock of the event wore off, reality began to set in. They were alive but still in great danger, with little fuel left in their petroleum lamps, no water, and no food. While no one spoke of it, they also knew they would eventually run out of air.

"A few members of the group proclaimed optimistically that rescue was probably on its way already, and there was nothing to worry about. The group was cheered by their claims that in only about twelve hours they would all be home safe and sound, reunited with their families. This positive approach to their dire situation was well-received, and everyone sat back and started to relax—save one, the oldest worker in the group.

"He said nothing but took a small hammer and started to chip away, not at the pile of debris on the caved-in path but at one of the untouched side walls. The others told him to stop, that help would arrive soon, but the man continued to chip and chisel small rocks out of the wall.

"Twelve hours came and went with no rescue in sight, not even the slightest noise from a possible attempt. Some of the group grew fearful their deliverance might not be as imminent as originally anticipated.

"The optimists in the group calmed the others down again, saying it had probably taken somewhat longer to organize the rescue team than they had figured, and they would surely be freed within the following twelve hours. The older man kept on quietly digging.

"The second twelve hours came and went with no sign of rescue, then another dozen hours and another. The group soon found themselves approaching seventy-two hours of being trapped deep in the earth. The petroleum lamps had long since flickered out, and the men sat huddled and freezing in complete darkness. They were growing weak from the cold, lack of water, and food. They all noticed the air had become thinner, making it more difficult to breathe.

"Panic set in again as they came to terms with their fate, followed by resignation. All gave up save the one who kept hammering away, even as they begged him to cease the useless effort and noise and let them have peace. Suddenly a cool breeze gushed into the chamber, and each man filled his lungs with a reviving breath of fresh air. It took a few seconds for them to realize what had happened. The old miner had broken through to a side tunnel! The group began to scream and hug each other as they realized rescue was indeed possible. And so it was. All seven made it out alive, gratefully hugging their families who waited topside at the elevator shaft. The media proclaimed it a miracle, as the search-and-rescue team had given up and declared them lost."

"What's that got to do with us?" Tom Murray broke the silence. "I'd say it was a lucky break and nothing more."

"Luck, Mr. Murray?" Dalton queried, tilting his head slightly to the side. "Really? Please allow me to finish the story."

The group turned eagerly back to Dalton.

"The mining village found itself in the worldwide spotlight. The town leaders held a festival in honor of the survivors, particularly lauding the man who never gave up and eventually brought about their rescue. During the festivities, a newspaper reporter convinced the hero to sit down for an interview.

"'How did you know there was a side tunnel?' the reporter asked.

"'I didn't,' the man responded.

"'But based on what the others said, you kept hammering as if you actually knew there was one.'

"'I had to keep myself busy,' he said simply.

"'How did you keep going for more than eighty hours when the rest of the team had given up and accepted that the end was near?' the reporter pressed.

"'You see,' the seasoned miner said, 'I was less optimistic than the rest of the group.'

"The reporter stopped writing on his notepad, pen poised over the paper, and looked at the man in confusion. 'You mean you were *more* optimistic,' he corrected.

"'No, sir. You heard me right. I was less optimistic.'

"'I don't understand.'

"'Being optimistic tends to be a short-term fix,' the man said. 'A few members of our group cheered the others on by convincing them every twelve hours that we would be rescued. As each deadline came and went, their optimism got weaker and weaker. We were in a dire situation, so I decided not to set any meaningless timelines.'

"'But I still don't get your comment about being less optimistic,' the reporter said.

"'I was not optimistic, sir. I hoped I would again see the light of day and embrace my wife and son. But what was more important was that I *believed* it was possible I could chip my way through to another tunnel within the time we had left before our air ran out. The twelve-hour rescue deadlines were based on nothing and set the others up for disappointment. Belief was my motivator. Believing we had the capacity to rescue ourselves kept me keep going.'"

Tom had no comeback and the rest of the group sat in silence, processing the metaphor.

Dalton declared a short break, and when they returned, he asked abruptly, "Who do you work for?"

"That's a rather naïve question, don't you think?" said Michelle Beckwith, somewhat annoyed.

"Not at all," Dalton replied. "In fact, it's extremely relevant to the next part of our conversation. How would you answer?"

"You've heard the opinions expressed here today. We work for a tyrant. We work for Mr. Ulrich," she said.

"Would anyone care to offer a different opinion?" Dalton asked.

"Hoppe Enterprises?" Karl Ruttner was rolling his eyes again.

"Let me rephrase the question," Dalton continued. "When you get up in the morning, who are you really going to work for?"

"We work for ourselves and our families," Joe Walt said, with conviction. The entire table turned to look at him. Walt had been uncharacteristically quiet throughout the entire discussion.

Dalton gently clapped his hands. "Excellent, Mr. Walt. Yes. You might be employed by a company, but the reason you go to work each day is clearly not for that company.

"No matter whether you are an administrative assistant, assembly line worker, director, vice president, or owner of the company, you do your job for the benefit of your family, yourself, and your future. Nothing will change that."

"Well, that's another way to look at it," Karen Singer said.

Dalton nodded. "The way you think becomes the way you feel, the way you feel translates into the way you act, and the way you act becomes your reality. As long as you think you work for a company, your life will be controlled by that organization. Once you realize you have bigger fish to fry, your perspective changes, and that shifts your reality.

"Confidence is born when you come to understand your true purpose, why you are doing what you are doing. When you then commit to that higher purpose, your commitment generates unlimited passion and gives meaning to your actions. I urge you to take a close look at what you are truly committed to. Such an examination will allow you to bring meaning back to what you are doing, and to see again how capable and powerful you really are."

Dalton stretched his arms over his head and bent slowly from side to side, then down to touch his toes and back up. "Now," he said,

"It's time for me to get on with my story. There is much ground yet to cover."

"Just a minute," Karl Ruttner interrupted. "I want to hear what Joe Walt has to say about all this talking owl business."

The group turned once again to look at Walt. He laced his hands behind his head and rocked far back in his chair, a mysterious grin on his face. "I'm going to keep an open mind," he said.

In Miss Dorothy's Sitting Room

I looked out the window and noticed it was getting dark. An hour or so earlier, Miss Dorothy had pulled back the draperies to allow Fabella to return to the woods behind the house. She had been talking for hours, but I was caught up in the story and did not interrupt her once. Now she paused for a long time, and I didn't know what to say.

"Did they?" I asked eventually.

"Did who do what?" she replied.

"Did they finish the *Arondight*?"

"Come, Robbie," Miss Dorothy said. "I think it's time for me to show you something."

We rose from the comfortable seats, and I took a double-step to keep from falling. My legs were stiff from sitting still for such a long time. I followed Miss Dorothy up the grand, curved staircase to the second floor of the house, which I had not previously been invited to visit.

A long hallway with a number of doors stretched to the right of the landing, which I deduced led to Miss Dorothy's private chambers. We turned to the left, where there was only a pair of heavy, carved wooden doors. Miss Dorothy swung them open and led me into what I thought at first was a large library. As I walked in, however, I realized it was more like a museum, filled with artifacts, antiques, and exhibits.

I was immediately drawn to a massive glass display case that took up most of the wall on the right-hand side of the room. Inside was the largest model sailboat I had ever seen, more than seven feet long and nearly ten feet from the keel to the tips of the masts. The blood-red sails gave the boat a regal aura, as if she were commanding the room. I could almost feel her energy.

"You asked if they ever finished it. See for yourself," Miss Dorothy said.

"Wow," was all I managed to mutter. "Absolutely amazing." I stared at the model for several minutes. I had been enthralled by Miss Dorothy's story from the beginning but seeing this made it all—real. Looking down, I noticed a brass plate affixed to the front of the display's base: *Arondight—Conqueror of the Seven Seas.*

A small, black-and-white photograph in an elegant frame sat on a little table next to the glass case. The picture had been bent at the edges and looked wallet-worn. Though the image was faded, I could make out a group of people standing next to the model boat. A sign hanging above them indicated they were in front of Jürgen's shop. Keagen's graduation day, I guessed, and they were all there.

Keagen himself was readily identifiable, as were Cassandra, his parents, and Sallie. Two other people I assumed to be Otto Jürgen and Mrs. Stockton. A cold shiver ran up my spine. I felt as if I knew each one of them and was looking at a group shot of my own best friends. I don't know how long I had been staring at the picture when I felt Miss Dorothy step to my side.

"She's really something, isn't she?"

"You can say that again. Just stunning," I replied.

Taking my arm, she said, "One more thing for you to see."

We walked to another tall table that held a glass cube on a marble base, softly lit from below. Within the cube rested a purple velvet cushion trimmed in red on which lay an open book.

Looking at it more closely, I saw that the pages were handwritten in elegant, formal-looking script. A brass plate on the front of the cube carried the inscription, *Seventy Summers, by Keagen Walkabee, Jr.*

"His memoirs," Miss Dorothy said. "Written by Keagen himself, one story at a time, one event at a time, encompassing most of his life. You have heard the beginning of this book today, minus the boardroom events of course, which happened more recently."

"You have just told me the story of that book?" I asked, baffled.

"The first part of it, yes. I've read this book so many times, I can tell it by heart."

"And there is more?" I asked eagerly.

"Yes, of course. There's much more to the story. In fact, we have just started."

"When do I get to hear the rest?"

She put her arm through mine again and began to walk me out. "It's getting late, and we are both tired. How about tomorrow? Shall we say, same time?"

"I'll be here. I can't wait."

As we approached the doors to the "museum room," a framed item on the wall caught my eye. It was an old, dirty, wrinkled fifty-dollar bill. Beneath it was written, in elegant calligraphy, *"You never lose your worth, no matter how you are being treated."*

"He didn't spend it after all," I thought. "Good for you, Keagen," I said aloud, softly. *"Good for you!"*

The streetlights were already on as I climbed into my Beetle for the drive home. I switched on the radio to relax and attempt to process the whole incredible day.

Miss Dorothy had spoken directly to my heart—it was as if she understood me better than anyone, though we had known each other only a short time. Keagen and his life seemed vividly real to me, and a good bit of his story might have been mine. I had the very clear sense I was on a journey and had just passed an important milestone regarding confidence and self-acceptance.

Metallica's "Nothing Else Matters" began blasting from the car's speakers. I turned it up even louder, rolled down the window, and let the wind blow through my hair as I sang along, entirely at peace, content and happy. I couldn't wait for what the next day might bring.

AUTHOR'S NOTE

On Confidence

During my years of traveling around the world conducting seminars on service excellence and leadership development, I've met thousands of people of all ranks, positions, and titles. And I'm always surprised by how quickly, how readily, many refer to themselves as "just." "Oh, I'm just an assistant manager." "I'm just an employee." The resignation and defeat evident in how they describe who they are and what they do is heartbreaking. I always wonder what the factors were that led to the "just"—not measuring up to a parent's or spouse's expectations, comparisons to friends and neighbors, not "living up to potential," feeling "not good enough."

During my research for this book, I discovered a poem that touched me deeply, as it seems to address this phenomenon. It was first presented at the 1979 National Parent Teacher Association (National PTA®) Convention.

The Average Child
I don't cause teachers trouble;
My grades have been okay.
I listen in my classes.
I'm in school every day.

My teachers think I'm average;
My parents think so, too.
I wish I didn't know that, though;
There's lots I'd like to do.
I would like to build a rocket;

I read a book on how.
Or start a stamp collection . . .
But no use trying now.

'Cause since I found I'm average,
I'm smart enough, you see,
To know there's nothing special
I should expect of me.

I'm part of that majority,
That hump part of the bell,
Who spends his life unnoticed
In an average kind of hell.

— Mike Buscemi

To anyone who has ever felt average, or second best, or second class, flunked a test, been bullied, been afraid to step out and be different, labeled a disappointment, suffered a broken relationship, had family troubles, or been subjected to any of the countless other storms life can throw at us, I have something important to tell you and some advice to impart. Never, ever speak of yourself as "just" anything. You *are* special; you are worth it all, a beautiful, creative being capable of things you haven't yet even dreamed of. You only need . . . confidence. The world needs you and wants you. Don't wait, though, because each of us only has about seventy summers.

God Bless!

Coming Soon: Seventy Summers, Book Two—Service

About the Authors

ANDY STANGENBERG is the founder and CEO of Q-Principle, which develops and delivers customized leadership and customer service training to companies in the global hospitality industry. He is also a sought-after keynote speaker who has addressed major conferences in more than a dozen countries on three continents. His training programs and motivational presentations focus on enterprise-wide service and leadership excellence and are based on his thirty-plus years of management experience in the hotel business. As a master business and life coach, Andy works with individuals and companies to improve the quality of their careers and their lives. He and his family live in Tacoma, Washington.

ANN WILSON is a writer, editor and communications consultant whose clients include Fortune 500 corporations and international associations as well as start-up enterprises and individual authors. She has won numerous awards for her clients for marketing programs, communications concepts and writing. She lives in Atlanta, Georgia.